TENDER TAKEOVER

To Sandy's dismay, she finds herself working for Oliver Carlton, the charismatic man who single-handedly destroyed her family — so when her hatred threatens to turn into something dangerously close to attraction, she uses all of her willpower to fight it. However, it swiftly becomes apparent that Oliver has romantic interests elsewhere, when Sandy catches sight of him with his arm around another woman . . .

SUSAN UDY

TENDER TAKEOVER

Complete and Unabridged

LINFORD
Leicester

First published in Great Britain in 2003

First Linford Edition
published 2014

A catalogue record for this book is available
from the British Library.

ISBN 978–1–4448–1831–4

Published by
F. A. Thorpe (Publishing)
Anstey, Leicestershire

Set by Words & Graphics Ltd.
Anstey, Leicestershire
Printed and bound in Great Britain by
T. J. International Ltd., Padstow, Cornwall

This book is printed on acid-free paper

1

Oliver Carlton strode purposefully into the offices of Meredith Engineering and Manufacturing. He was dressed immaculately, if conservatively, in a dark blue suit, white shirt and pale blue silk tie. He looked every inch the successful, self-made businessman that he was.

Sandra Owen, known to most as Sandy, stopped what she was doing for just long enough to glance up at the clock on the wall. Four o'clock.

She tightened her lips. Hardly worth bothering to show up at all, she would have thought. In the three weeks since he'd taken over the company, Oliver had only been in twice, each time arriving late in the afternoon, to remain only for as long as it took to issue a string of commands to Sandy before leaving again.

Mind you, to give him his due, the Christmas break had been largely instrumental in this poor attendance record. Nonetheless, such behaviour seemed to bear out his reputation for acquiring a business and then leaving whichever management team he'd seen fit to appoint or retain to get on with things.

Sandy was one of the original team he'd retained, albeit in a much superior position. To say she'd been astonished when he'd offered her the job of his Personal Assistant and chief adviser on all aspects of Meredith's business would be an understatement of quite major proportions. In fact, she'd been positively stunned.

He now barely broke his stride as he said, 'Would you come to my office, San — '

Sandy's brow lowered in a frown.

'Um, Ms Owen?' he finished.

Sandy smiled grimly to herself. Hell would have to have frozen over before she'd consent to Oliver Carlton addressing her as Sandy! Clearly, he'd picked up on that sentiment. Just as well, because

she fully intended to keep this relation-
ship on a purely professional basis, for
as long as she stayed at Meredith's, that
was.

As soon as another job, with equal
status and pay came along, she would
be off and then she'd never have to set
eyes on him again. As it was, she had
to brace herself every morning to come to
the office, fearful of whatever dealings
she might be forced to have with the
man who had single-handedly destroyed
her family.

'Certainly, Mr Carlton.'

She rearranged her features so that
no indication of her revulsion for him
should show and stood up, picking up
her notepad as she did so.

'You won't be needing that,' Oliver
said pointedly.

Sandy tightened her lips once more. He
was so arrogant, so totally self-assured.
He was also annoyingly good-looking,
tall, six feet one or two, she would
guess, with dark hair and eyes to match,
a straight, almost aquiline nose, a

chiselled jawline, and a well-shaped mouth. But beneath those charismatic looks, she knew there ran a vein of utter ruthlessness. There would have to be, to induce him to do what he'd done to her father.

She glanced at June, her own personal secretary, another promotion. June raised her eyebrows. Good grief! Sandy almost groaned aloud with despair. Even the normally sensible June was smitten! Sandy ignored the look and, stiff-backed with resentment at what she was being forced to submit to, followed Oliver Carlton into his office.

'Take a seat, please, Ms Owen.'

Was it her imagination, Sandy wondered, or did he stress the formal title?

'I'm glad to see you're dressed smartly.'

Sandy was startled into a sharp retort.

'What did you expect me to come to work in? Sweatshirt and denims?'

A glimmer of a smile made its

appearance upon the handsome face. Just for a second, Sandy felt her heart miss a beat.

'Hardly,' he replied and as he spoke, his gaze appraised her long, honey-blonde hair, her grey eyes, her pert, ever-so-slightly tip-tilted nose, her mouth, to linger with frank appreciation upon her suit-clad figure.

Sandy practically squirmed in her seat. His remark, however, when he made it, was perfectly innocuous.

'What I meant was that you are dressed appropriately for the meeting I've arranged for us.'

His statement drove all else from her mind.

'Meeting? Now?'

It was gone four o'clock. Working hours were eight till four thirty, even for the office staff, although it wasn't uncommon for Sandy to stay late, when her workload demanded it.

'At Crockets, with Burton, the work's manager. They want their manufacturing division completely redesigned and refitted, all new machinery and plant. You told me you invariably assisted Tony Hatchard with that sort of thing, so I would welcome your expertise and input.'

Assisted Tony? Sandy almost snorted with derision. She practically did the whole thing, single-handedly. Admittedly, Tony came up with the rudiments of the design, but it had always been left to Sandy to carry the job through, from the initial planning stage to the overseeing of the manufacturing and delivery of the finished product.

Tony Hatchard had much preferred to be out on the golf course. She suspected, although he hadn't said as much, that Oliver Carlton knew this, which would explain him getting rid of Tony and elevating Sandy.

'Be ready to leave in five minutes. I said we'd be there at around five thirty, six at the latest.'

'Where are we meeting Mr Burton?'

'I've just said, at Crockets.'

'But that's in Manchester, too far to

drive in an hour or so.'

'We're not going by car.'

She snorted.

'Well, we certainly won't make it by train.'

'We won't be using the train either.'

Sandy couldn't be sure but she thought she detected traces of amusement in his tone. Disconcertingly, it made him seem almost human, rather than the cold-hearted hatchet man that his reputation had him down as. For the second time, her heart skipped a beat. Determined not to be swayed by this, she snapped out her reply, aware of maybe going too far but past caring, if the truth were know.

'So, how are we getting there? Carrier pigeon?'

'Close,' Oliver murmured smoothly.

Strangely enough, he didn't seem at all put out by her waspishness, which again seemed to fly in the face of the way that rumour and gossip had depicted him. Sandy was beginning to feel confused. She'd expected anger in response to her provocative question, an irritated put-down, at the very least.

So what was all this? A deliberate ploy? A sort of keep-them-on-edge tactic, uncertain, and so win the game? She wouldn't put it past him. From all she'd heard this man would be capable of anything, short of murder, that is. And in her father's case, he could almost be accused of that, but she mustn't go down that road, not now, not here. Oliver's voice dragged her back to the present.

'Plane,' he said coolly.

Sandy blinked at him.

'Plane?'

'Uh-huh.'

He snapped his brief-case shut, after checking he had everything he needed.

'I've chartered a private plane, from the local airfield. A friend of mine runs a service for businessmen.'

'How very convenient,' she bit out.

'Yes, I find it so. Now, are you ready to go?'

Sandy regarded him as if he'd taken

leave of his senses.

'But I can't fly off, just like that.'

'Really? Why not? We should be back again by mid-evening. If you have plans — '

'I don't,' she interrupted.

Oliver raised a knowing eyebrow.

'Oh, I see. You think I should have consulted you first, before arranging things?'

'Well, it would have been nice, not to say courteous and considerate.'

Oliver grinned at that. It wasn't an amused grin this time, however. It was a heavily sardonic one.

'It would have been nice,' he mimicked.

Sandy simmered, only just managing to restrain herself from walking out, right there and then. She'd been forced more than once in recent weeks to tell herself that she needed this job, for a while, at least. She couldn't blow things now, not till she'd found herself another position somewhere; then, and only then, would she be free to tell Oliver

9

Carlton exactly what she thought of him.

'I don't do business that way, Ms Owen.'

There was a distinct edge to his voice now.

'I thought I'd made that clear when I offered you the position of my PA and chief adviser. I expect you to be ready to go with me at a moment's notice. That's why I pay you so well.'

'Well, yes, I realise that.'

She did recall him saying something to that effect during their initial interview. However, she hadn't expected to have to be on call twenty four hours a day.

'But my family will be expecting me back.'

'Ring them.'

His steel gaze told her that he wasn't making a suggestion, he was issuing an order.

Stung by his air of undisputed authority over her, and knowing that she had no choice but to do as he said,

Sandy snatched up the phone, at the same time punching in her home number. It was a gesture of fury, the only one she felt able to make.

Sandy's mother, Felicity, answered the phone.

'It's me, Mum.'

Sandy went on to tell her where she was going, as briefly and as calmly as she could, all the time aware of her employer's gaze.

'Flying to Manchester? Now? But there's snow forecast for this evening, darling. Quite a lot, apparently. Are you sure it's a wise decision, to go today? Couldn't it wait?'

'It's not my decision, Mother.'

'Well, whose is it? Not that wretched man's surely. Tell him from me — '

Sandy decided it was time to cut the call short. Oliver Carlton was starting to look more than a little irritated. Could he hear what her mother was saying? Felicity had been speaking loudly, as she always did when indignant about something.

If he had heard, the description of himself as that wretched man wouldn't go down at all well.

'Got to go. I'll see you later,' she said hastily. 'I'm not sure when. If there's a problem, I'll let you know.'

Thoughtfully, she replaced the receiver and then turned to look at Oliver Carlton. She was very hard pressed indeed to hide her emotions, but the truth was that for the very first time in her limited dealings with him, she felt that she had the upper hand, and she could barely suppress her triumph.

However, it wouldn't do to let him know that, not yet, so she rearranged her features into something that she hoped indicated nothing more than good-natured interest.

'Have you checked the weather forecast?' she asked. 'There's going to be some snow, apparently, heavy snow. Several inches, in fact.'

She deliberately laid it on thickly, as thickly as the snow that was forecast. Now let him say they'd still go.

'Yes, I know.'

Disappointingly, he looked totally unfazed. He didn't even take the trouble to look at her as he spoke. He'd opened his briefcase again and was searching through it.

Sandy felt a hot stab of anger. Was nothing capable of puncturing this man's arrogance, his sheer confidence — not even the prospect of several inches of snow on an airport runway? Or did he think if he ignored it, it would simply go away? Or maybe not arrive in the first place?

'It shouldn't be enough to prevent us from going. Now, are you ready?'

He was looking at her again, a glint of something in his tawny eye. Anticipation? Amusement again? Or was it that he simply enjoyed sparring with her? It seemed an unlikely notion, yet there was something. Whatever the expression signified, she couldn't deny that it intensified his charismatic looks.

Sandy felt her breath catch in her throat. If she didn't hate him quite so much, she could imagine being as smitten as the rest of Meredith's female staff. However, thankfully, she did hate him, so no danger of that.

'Not really,' she snapped, 'but it seems I have no choice in the matter.'

'That's right,' he quipped, 'you don't.'

2

Although they landed at Manchester in a snowstorm, it wasn't serious enough to prevent the car that was waiting for them outside the airport from reaching Crockets. Sadly, by the time they were ready to leave there once more, it was a different story. The roads were completely obliterated and a virtual blizzard was raging.

Sandy listened with growing dismay to Oliver's end of the phone conversation with the pilot. Then he turned to her after switching off his mobile.

'No chance of getting home tonight,' he said and she suspected that her face, always so painfully transparent, would be registering every scrap of her horror.

As her dealings with him were beginning to demonstrate, Oliver was far too astute not to have recognised her expression for what it was, which made it all the more strange that all he should say was a casual, 'We'll have to book into a hotel. I think I noticed a Novatel about half a mile up the road.'

Sandy was speechless. The thought of having to spend a second longer than necessary in his company was enough to turn her blood as cold as the snow thickening in front of her.

'But I can't do that. I've got no overnight things with me,' she protested.

'Neither have I. Don't worry.'

His voice was as smooth as his look.

'There's bound to be a shop inside, in reception. We'll buy whatever we need.'

The driver of the hire car managed to slither and slide his way to the hotel without serious mishap and, sure enough, it was almost exactly half a mile up the road.

Trust Oliver Carlton to be right, Sandy thought in disgust. Was he ever wrong? Mind you, he'd been wrong about the weather. That reflection gave her no satisfaction at all, because the very last thing she wanted was to be forced to spend time with him, but maybe he wouldn't want that either. After all, she was simply an employee.

She couldn't envisage him putting himself out to entertain her. No, a much more likely prospect was her eating a meal alone and then opting for an early night. That thought provided her with some comfort, at least.

Once he'd checked them both in, Oliver pointed out the small shop in the far corner of the reception area of the hotel.

'Buy whatever you need and charge it to my room, or if you'd rather, pay for it and the company will reimburse you.'

Up in her room, the first thing Sandy did was ring her mother.

'Oh, darling,' her mother cried, 'if you can't get home, what will you do? This is all that man's fault.'

'I'm in a hotel.'

'Not with him!'

Her mother sounded appalled.

'I have no other choice, Mother.

Hopefully the snow will have eased by morning and I'll be able to get back.'

After managing to convince her mother that she was in no immediate danger from that man, she hung up and ran herself a bath. The hotel supplied some rather up-market bath foam. She emptied the bottle into the running water. That would have to do instead of perfume, although why she felt the need for perfume of any description, she couldn't have said. After all, she'd already convinced herself that she'd be dining alone.

She'd managed to purchase some make-up and toiletries as well as a complete set of underwear. She'd drawn the line at anything else, although they had a very tempting line in designer outfits! Her suit would have to do for this evening as well as tomorrow.

She'd have her bath and go down for an early meal, and that way she should manage to avoid her employer. The room sported satellite TV so she'd come back here and watch a film of some sort.

It wasn't to be!

The phone by the side of the bed rang. She frowned at it. It could only be Oliver Carlton. Should she ignore it? But even as she had the thought, her hand was reaching for the receiver. She lifted it to her ear.

'Meet me in the Mulberry Bar in half an hour. We may as well eat together.'

Sandy slammed the phone back down. The cheek of the man! Did he possess no social skills at all?

'Maybe I should give him a lesson or two in the art of making a woman feel wanted,' she muttered as she walked into the bathroom and climbed into the frothy, highly-scented water.

She wrinkled her nose. Had she overdone it? She didn't want to go downstairs smelling like one of those women who stood waving their perfume sample bottles around in department stores. Why hadn't she said no to Oliver, as she had originally intended?

Instead, for some unknown reason, she'd heard herself saying, 'OK, in half an hour,' as meek as you like.

She couldn't believe it. She hated the man, didn't she? Yes, of course she did. However, she couldn't afford to offend him, not yet. Her mother and sister were totally dependent on her for their livelihoods.

Still angry with herself, for all her sensible reasoning, she eventually climbed from the bath and put on her suit once more. She grimaced at her reflection in the mirror. It was very creased, but well, it would have to do. And if Mr Oliver Carlton didn't like it, too bad! It was his fault they were stuck here, when all was said and done.

Oliver's gaze raked over her as she joined him, probably counting the creases, one by one, she reflected acrimoniously. He made no comment, although he must have noticed.

'Your room to your liking?'

He was politeness itself, which only infuriated Sandy all the more. He couldn't be looking forward to spending the entire evening with an employee. Why couldn't he have been open and above board about it and simply left her to her own devices? It had been what she was expecting, after all.

'It's fine.'

Actually it was far superior to anything that she'd ever been used to but she wasn't about to tell him that.

They had a drink in the bar and then went to the dining-room. Sandy was relieved to have something to occupy herself with, even if it was just the menu. Up till then, the conversation had been polite, if a little stilted. She wasn't used to mixing socially with the likes of Oliver Carlton and she was quite sure he wasn't accustomed to mixing with the likes of her.

She smiled grimly to herself. She'd heard he was a very wealthy man, well, he must be to buy up companies like he did. Meredith's wasn't the first. One other in particular, Sandy knew about. It stuck in her mind like the proverbial beacon.

Her father had worked there, and

Oliver Carlton Enterprises had moved in and snapped up the ailing firm. It had taken him and his team just twenty-four hours to go through the employees with a chainsaw. Her father and thirty eight others had been made redundant.

In her father's case, it was with the minimum payment the law required and the order to leave the building at once. As her father had been Company Secretary and Head Accountant, this had been somewhat unusual. Others had been paid much more, although, in the main, they, too, had been told to leave at once.

It had completely destroyed Martin Owen. Two days after that he'd tried to take his own life. If Sandy hadn't arrived home early and found him, he would surely have died. As it was, the paramedics she'd called administered emergency treatment and the local hospital managed to save him.

None of that helped Martin, however. He sank daily into a deeper and deeper depression until a workmate who'd also been made redundant bought a small bar in Spain and offered Martin a job as barman, with a partnership in the offing when they started to make a decent profit. Martin would have bought in straight away but the family needed his meagre redundancy money, not least to pay the mortgage with.

'A month or two,' he'd promised Felicity, Sandy and Lucy, the youngest daughter, 'then I'll send for you all.'

He'd been completely oblivious to his daughters' stricken faces, especially sixteen-year-old Lucy.

'I want to go to college here, not in Spain,' she'd cried.

However, it didn't come to that. The promised two months turned into three, then four, and then five. His letters and phone calls became fewer before, finally, they stopped altogether. Felicity was frantic, convinced something awful had happened. She was all for flying out to Spain but Sandy first rang the bar where he'd been working and spoke to the owner.

'He just took off, luv, two weeks ago. I'm no wiser than you. We had a bit of a row. He was pressing for the partnership but there was no way I could offer him one, even if he could afford to put in some money. I'm just not making enough for both of us to take a substantial income out. We'd have gone broke. As I said, we had a row and he just took off. I haven't heard from him since.'

Sandy informed the police of his disappearance and asked the bar owner to do the same in Spain, mainly because Felicity was frightened he might have tried to commit suicide again. But nothing more was heard of him. It was as if Martin Owen had disappeared off the face of the earth.

It wasn't long after that that the redundancy money ran out and they were forced to sell their large house for considerably less than it was worth, so making barely any money on it at all. They moved into a small, rented property. Sandy, as sole wage earner, was the one who paid. That had been twelve months ago.

From that time on, the family had been united in their condemnation of Oliver Carlton and now, here was Sandy being forced to work for him. Felicity had complained bitterly when she'd told her who had taken over, as had Lucy.

'How can you work for that callous monster? But for him, our father would still be here. Have you no conscience?'

To which Sandy's level-headed response had been, 'If I don't work, we don't live. We don't have a roof over our heads. Is that what you want?'

'No, of course it isn't, darling,' Felicity had put in swiftly. 'But is there no other way? It seems like such a betrayal of your father.'

'No, Mother, for the present there is no other way, not until I can find another job that pays as well, anyway.'

She had turned back to her glowering sister.

'And if you want to continue at

college instead of getting a job, Lucy, then you'll have to put up with it.'

And look where her sensible approach had got her! Sitting opposite the callous monster, eating dinner! Goodness knows what Lucy was going to say. But, unexpectedly, with those first uncomfortable moments over with, the evening turned into quite a pleasant one.

The monster revealed his more human side. It was even a faintly likeable one. Sandy had caught a couple of glimpses of it already but now it was on full display. So much so, that at one point, she found herself wondering if he was really as black as his reputation painted him. She caught herself up at that. Of course he was. This was just his crafty way of manipulating her.

She had all the proof she needed of his ruthlessness, his complete self-absorption. She owed it to her father to remain on her guard, to go on hating him, no matter what.

There was one sticky moment when Oliver asked her to tell him about her family. It was quite clear that he didn't have the foggiest notion of who she was. Of course, Owen was a pretty common surname and it was more than likely that Oliver had completely forgotten a man called Martin Owen, if he'd ever known him. As she recalled, it hadn't been Oliver personally who'd done the dirty deed with regards to her father, it had been one of his minions. Somehow, that had made it even worse.

So, opting for the least contentious path, Sandy had limited her reply to a casual, 'There's just three of us, myself, my mother and my younger sister, Lucy.'

She did wonder fleetingly how he'd react if she should be bold enough to say, 'My father has disappeared, mainly due to your disgraceful treatment of him.'

As if he'd picked up her thoughts, he asked, 'No father?'

Sandy's expression must have betrayed her distress because he immediately went on.

'Sorry, that was clumsy of me. Tell me about your mother and sister. What do they do?'

'My mother takes care of us and my sister is studying art and design at college.'

Oliver was watching her intently, she noticed.

'So, you're the sole breadwinner. A big responsibility for one so young.'

'Young? I'm twenty-six.'

'I see. Positively antique then.'

His subsequent grin was an infectious one and Sandy found herself smiling back, only to receive a rather odd response. Oliver looked taken aback.

'You should do that more often.'

He was still watching her, but now it was from beneath hooded eyelids. Sandy was puzzled, both by his reaction and his words.

'Do what?'

'Smile. It suits you.'

It was Sandy's turn to appear disconcerted. Anyone would think she never laughed, although, she probably hadn't in Oliver Carlton's company until now.

'I don't often have much to smile about. Now, if you'll excuse me, I think I'll go to bed.'

'Good idea. I think I'll join you.'

Sandy was acutely conscious of the rush of blood to her face. He couldn't mean what that sounded like!

'Don't look so horrified. What I mean is, I'll go to bed as well, in my own room.'

Sandy's blush deepened.

'Oh, I didn't think — '

'Didn't you? You could have fooled me then.'

He paused.

'Would it be so terrible? I hadn't thought myself quite as repulsive as your expression would seem to imply.'

His tone was a harsh one and sardonic to the point of rudeness. Sandy, caught off guard by his blunt way of talking, began to stutter.

'I — um, didn't mean — um, I

shouldn't have — '

Oh, no! Now, she sounded like some sort of naïve adolescent. Talk about blotting her copybook on their first joint business trip! Whatever must he be thinking?

She was soon to find out. He left her in no doubt of his opinion of her faux pas.

'Believe me, Ms Owen, there are more than enough eager candidates for the position of my mistress to ensure that I don't have to attempt to coerce a patently unwilling woman. I'll see you in the morning. Be ready to leave at first light. Sleep well.'

And with that, he rose from the table and strode away without as much as a backward glance, leaving Sandy still red-faced and squirming with embarrassment and humiliation, and fervently praying that no-one else had overheard their astringent little exchange.

3

To Sandy's relief, when she glanced out of the window the following morning, she saw that the snow had turned to rain overnight, leaving the roads clear once more. It was as if there'd never been a blizzard.

Reluctantly, she went downstairs to breakfast — and Oliver Carlton. She was in dread of how he would behave with her after the previous evening's fiasco. She'd obviously angered him.

However, all he said was a curt, 'Good morning. Did you sleep well?'

Sandy replied, equally abruptly, 'Yes, thank you.'

They ate breakfast and then travelled back to the factory in more or less total silence. Oliver then immersed himself in papers he pulled from his briefcase while Sandy busied herself jotting down copious notes to remind her of the exact details and estimated costings of the plant that Crockets had asked for. The order seemed a firm one but would, obviously, hinge on the final written quotation from Meredith's.

Within an hour of being back, Sandy felt as if she'd never been away. Oliver had, right from their first moment of meeting that morning, reverted to type. So much so, that Sandy was convinced she'd imagined his warmer, more human side. Even so, she couldn't believe it when he walked into her office and dumped a pile of work upon her, enough to keep her going for at least a week.

'By tomorrow, please,' he requested, only adding insult to injury.

'Right.'

Sandy simmered furiously. What did he think she was? A human computer, capable of carrying out a dozen different tasks all at once?

'I'll be out for the rest of the day,' he went on. 'We're scheduled to visit Custer's tomorrow afternoon, same sort of thing as yesterday, a quote for a factory refit with automated production line. I'll need you with me again. Also, make sure that Bill Hopkins is free to meet us there. I would expect to need him for the technical side of things.'

'Yes, sir, three bags full, sir,' Sandy muttered under her breath.

How was she supposed to do the pile of work he'd presented her with and go to Custer's?

Once he'd gone, she said to June, 'Work can wait for ten minutes. I'm going to get a sandwich. Do you want anything?'

'I'll go if you like.'

June's glance rested doubtfully on the pile of files and papers which Oliver had deposited on Sandy's desk.

'You're going to be busy.'

'It's OK. I need the fresh air.'

She was halfway across Meredith's carpark when she was all but knocked over by a small, yellow sports car. If raced through the carpark entrance and screeched to a sliding halt just beyond

Sandy, splashing her in the process with filthy, slushy water. In the same instant, the driver's door flew open and a pair of shapely legs protruded, to be followed immediately by an equally shapely body.

Despite the fact that she was bent practically double, making futile attempts to dry her splattered legs with a paper handkerchief, Sandy recognised the woman instantly. She'd have to be blind not to. Stunningly attractive, she was a well known sight around the town, more often than not, in the company of some handsome man.

She was Portia Hollis, the daughter of the local estate agent who'd sold the Owen home in the aftermath of Martin's disappearance. Whatever was she doing in Meredith's carpark? Sandy didn't have to wait long to find out.

As she watched, Portia waved an arm in the air and called, 'Oliver, over here.'

Sandy didn't mean to stare but she simply couldn't help herself. She wanted to see how well Oliver and this lovely woman knew each other. By the way that Oliver went straight to her and put an arm about her waist, it was very well indeed. He then led her to his own car, a top of the range model.

Sandy dabbed at her legs a couple of times more, not that it improved matters, and then straightened up. No wonder he'd administered such a put-down to Sandy the evening before. Why would he want her for company when he could clearly have the gorgeous Portia? None of her thoughts explained why Sandy should feel so depressed as she continued on her way to the sandwich bar.

It wasn't until after lunch the following day that Oliver arrived back in the office. Why was he involving himself in the day-to-day running of Meredith's, Sandy couldn't imagine. From what she'd heard, it wasn't something he normally did. Could it be that he didn't trust the management here? Or was it her, Sandy, whom he didn't trust? He couldn't be accustomed to his employees answering him back the way she did.

'Are you ready, Ms Owen?'

'Quite ready, Mr Carlton.'

'Did you finish those figures and employee details I asked for?'

'No.'

To her vexation, Sandy felt her face colouring. She hardly ever blushed. What was it about this man that he should have such an effect upon her?

'I wasn't sure what time you'd be here. You didn't tell me yesterday, apart from saying afternoon.'

It was a fairly pointed rebuke.

'You'll have them later, if we aren't too long at Custer's.'

One eyebrow winged up his forehead. It was a trick that Sandy was beginning to recognise, and it seemed to signal irritation, or could it be scepticism at what she'd said?

'Fine. Let's go then. You'll be eager to get back,' he said abruptly.

'Quite so,' Sandy replied icily.

Custer's was situated on an industrial estate some five miles out of Wilmsley, a ten-minute drive away.

'We'll go in my car,' Oliver said, taking hold of her arm and leading her in that direction.

'Wouldn't it be better if I simply followed in mine?' Sandy asked. 'Then you wouldn't have to bring me back, if you've got other plans for the rest of the day.'

What she meant was, if he was meeting the gorgeous Portia again.

'I haven't got other plans. Get in.'

Did he have to be so arrogant, Sandy wondered.

'Get in,' she silently mimicked.

A 'please' would have been nice. Really, his mother should have taught him some manners!

'I want to show you something. We've got time.'

Time for what? Sandy's curiosity was well and truly aroused. She didn't have to wait long for the answer. Within minutes, they were driving through the high gates of Wilmsley Prior, the oldest as well as the largest house in the village.

'Are we going to see the Millingtons?' she asked.

'No, they're not here. I've got the keys. They've just put the house on the market.'

'Have they?'

Sandy regarded him in astonishment.

'They've kept that very quiet, amazing in a place the size of Wilmsley. People usually know when you've sneezed more than twice.'

Oliver gave her a sideways grin. His mood seemed to have improved and once again he was showing her his warmer side. Clearly, he was able to switch moods at a second's notice. It was extremely disconcerting, unnerving, even.

'They didn't want a board outside. They're having to move for financial reasons.'

'How did you know about it?'

'I've met Portia Hollis. She knew I was looking for somewhere in this vicinity so she tipped me the wink. I've already been to have a look. I believe you saw us together. She was taking me to view it.'

So he had seen her, watching them the previous day, for all her efforts to appear wholly intent upon the business of cleaning herself up. She'd wondered about that. He'd given no sign that he'd spotted her.

'I would value your opinion, as someone impartial.'

'Well, I'm not really up on what's a good buy or not.'

'I don't mean that. I want a woman's viewpoint. Would you live here? Would it make a suitable family home? That sort of thing.'

'Couldn't Portia have provided that? She is a woman, after all,' Sandy concluded drily.

'She's also trying to sell it to me.'

He did have a point. Sandy slanted a glance at him. He must be thinking of getting married, again. He'd been married once before, fifteen or sixteen years ago she'd found out. It hadn't lasted long. He'd only been twenty-three at the time, at least, that's what she'd heard on the factory grapevine, which, if it was correct, would make him thirty eight or nine now. He'd done well for a relatively young man. He'd amassed quite a fortune if he could afford this place.

It stood three storeys high and possessed a wealth of mullioned windows. She'd never actually been in here before and it could barely be seen from the road, protected as it was by a high perimeter beech hedge and iron railings.

Oliver brought the car to a halt before the impressive front entrance. Immediately above it, there was a huge, stained-glass window that stretched up through most of the top two floors.

'It needs a bit of renovation as you can see, mainly a paint job and maybe some repointing of the brickwork. The roof's in good nick, so, nothing too extreme. The work shouldn't take long. It's important to me that I retain the character and charm of the historic place.'

'I see.'

Yet again, he was revealing a more sensitive, more humane side to his nature, which, given his reputation for ruthlessness, was unexpected, to say the least. She had to concede he'd only got rid of some half a dozen of the Meredith employees and most of them had been near retirement, apart from Tony, that was. Maybe he was mellowing as he got older.

Thoughtfully, she followed Oliver inside, into a large, square, black-and-white tiled hallway. A magnificent, stone stairway curved out of this to the upper floor.

'How many bedrooms?' she enquired.

'Ten.'

So, if he was indeed to marry, he must be planning a large family! Images came to her then of several golden-haired children playing in the hall, perhaps a couple of dogs, and a woman — Portia Hollis?

Oliver led her all over the house. It was just as she would have expected, perfectly-proportioned rooms, all with high ceilings, quite a few of them with their original beams intact and uncovered, cavernous fireplaces. Sandy would give her eye teeth to live here. When they were back in the hallway again, he turned to her.

'So, what do you think?' he asked.

He was observing her so intently, Sandy felt as if her views really mattered. Why? Why did Oliver Carlton care whether she liked the house or not?

'I think you've got visitors.'

He looked puzzled.

'Mice!' she replied. 'Can't you smell them, especially in here?'

'I thought it was damp. That's what I've asked the surveyor to check for.'

'It could be that as well, but I can definitely smell mice.'

She sniffed again, turning her head this way and that, leaning forward, pointing towards the skirting boards.

'They could be behind there. There are several small holes and cracks.'

'You're an expert on mice then, are

you?' he asked, sounding amused.

Sandy's own mouth curved into a grin.

'We had them at home, a couple of years ago.'

As she spoke, there was a rustling sound in the corner and a small brown creature darted out, to scamper virtually over her feet, and disappear down one of the small holes that she'd pointed out in the skirting board. She squealed, leaping sideways, straight into Oliver.

Oliver didn't hesitate. After an initial sideways stagger as he absorbed the impact of her body, he slid his arms about her, lacing his fingers together at the back of her waist, effectively imprisoning her in his embrace.

'Well, well, this is unexpected,' he drawled, still with a broad grin.

Sandy felt extremely foolish and immediately set about trying to pull herself free, but Oliver simply tightened his hold upon her.

'S — sorry,' she stammered.

'Don't be. It was quite delightful. Are there any more to come, do you think?'

With an exaggerated look of anxiety, he glanced around the hallway. Sandy was hard-pressed not to laugh. He was teasing her. She couldn't imagine Oliver Carlton being apprehensive about anything, let alone a single, solitary mouse.

However, she was decidedly apprehensive, of being so close to him. It was provoking all sorts of odd and totally unexpected responses within her. For starters, she could feel his breath feathering the top of her head, which was prompting a shivery, weak feeling inside her. The smell of his aftershave invaded her nostrils, filling her head and making it swim. She closed her eyes, dizzy with the effort of maintaining some semblance of composure.

'I sincerely hope there are no more,' she managed to say finally, 'or, at least, if there are, let's hope it's your feet they run over this time.'

Even to her own ears, her voice sounded strained and nervous. Oliver must have noticed. However, if he did, he gave no sign of it.

'I thought you were accustomed to the sight of mice?' he simply said.

'I might be accustomed to them, but that's not to say I want them running over my feet,' she replied shakily. 'Not that I'm that frightened of them,' she hastily assured him.

It was the wrong thing to say.

'So, if it's not the mice you're scared of, you're not frightened of me, are you? You're trembling.'

There was a very strange look to him now, an almost anticipatory look, wolfish, even. The tawny eyes gleaming at her. Sandy felt her cheeks growing warm again. Her awareness of this provoked a waspish retaliation from her.

'Of course not.'

Somehow, she had to pull herself back together, not an easy task beneath his watchful eye.

'It was the shock, that's all. I wasn't expecting it to run that close, or to run at all, come to that, not with us here.'

Really, the conceit of the man. Why should he think she was frightened of him? She wasn't frightened exactly, more disturbed. It was the first time they'd been that close and, undoubtedly, it was his proximity that was responsible for her powerful reaction. Such a thing had never happened before, not with any other man, and the fact that she'd resolved to hate him, come what may, made what had happened to her seem all the more shameful.

From now on, she'd make sure she maintained a safe distance between them. She didn't want a repeat performance. That reflection was more than enough to imbue her with the will to free herself and she smiled with saccharine sweetness up at him.

'It seems to have gone to ground again so you can let go of me now.'

For a moment, he made no move to release her. Sandy wondered why, and then an odd notion occurred to her. If she didn't know him for the cold, calculating monster that he really was, she could almost believe he was enjoying holding her so close.

By the time they'd eventually been to Custer's and returned to the offices, it was getting late, and Sandy still had that work to do that Oliver wanted finished.

'I'll drop you here,' Oliver said, just pulling inside the entrance to the carpark. 'I've got another appointment.'

With Portia Hollis, Sandy wondered. He'd said earlier he had nothing planned for later. She wondered if he'd rung her while they'd been at Custer's. He hadn't been with Sandy all of the time so it was possible.

He'd quizzed her about her opinion of the house on their drive to Custer's.

'I think it's gorgeous,' she'd told him, 'but maybe a bit large for one person.'

'Who says it's for one person?'

'Oh, well, I assumed — '

'I'm hoping to marry, in the not-too-distant future.'

Sandy had made no reply to that. So, she'd been right. Still, it was none of her business. He could do whatever he liked, in which case, she'd asked herself furiously, why the strange feeling in the pit of her stomach?

4

Sandy remained preoccupied for quite some time after that, even while she carried on with her work. She didn't understand what was happening to her. For all the warmth and humour that Oliver Carlton had so unexpectedly shown her, it was unthinkable that she could be, in anyway, attracted to him. Despite what her senses had been trying to tell her, not after what he'd done to her father.

She was so determined to have the work done that evening that she was still at her desk at eight o'clock. Everyone else had long gone so she was quite alone when the door opened unexpectedly behind her and Oliver strode in.

Her expression must have revealed her alarm because he quickly said, 'Sorry, did I startle you?'

'A bit, yes. I thought I was the only person here.'

'You were. I was passing and saw the light on so I thought I'd just check that everything was OK.'

His gaze went to the papers on her desk.

'You're surely not working this late?'

'You said you needed these reports and figures.'

'Oh, tomorrow would have done to complete them.'

'Now he tells me,' she muttered under her breath.

'Did you say something?'

'No.'

'Come on then. You've done enough for today. Working this late goes well beyond the call of duty. I'll buy you dinner as a reward for being so conscientious. And, after all, it was me who delayed us this afternoon by dragging you along to Wilmsley Prior.'

He gave her yet another engaging smile — in vain. Sandy was busy steeling herself to withstand his deliberate appeal. He wasn't going to be allowed to affect her as he had earlier, no way. But why was he suddenly going out of his way to charm her, because he undoubtedly was? Could it be that he just couldn't bear the notion that he was failing where she was concerned?

She would hazard a guess that he wasn't used to being turned down, by any woman, never mind his personal assistant. Well, if that was the reason, he was going to have to do a darned sight more than just smile to win her around.

'Sorry, my mother's expecting me back. She'll have cooked me something.'

She got to her feet and walked to the coatstand.

'Ring her. Surely she'll understand.'

Oliver lifted the receiver of the phone and held it out to her. Sandy took it and equally deliberately replaced it.

'No, I've still got a few more things to add to the staff report. I'll do it at home.'

'I've just told you,' he said in a voice ominously low, 'sometime tomorrow will do.'

51

She met his look with no little difficulty. His eyes had darkened and hardened and his mouth had thinned to an inflexible slit, which only seemed to bear out her theory that he wasn't accustomed to being denied that which he wanted. For some inexplicable reason, he wanted to dine with her. She felt her resolve to stand out against him begin to weaken.

'But I understood them to be urgent.'

'Not that urgent that you have to work all evening.'

'Well,' she said as she slid her arms into her coat, still determined to resist him, 'I'd still rather finish while things are fresh in my mind.'

She picked up her handbag and began to walk from the office. All she had to do was stand firm, keeping saying no. In the end, he'd have to take the hint, wouldn't he? But apparently not. He followed her out.

'I'll walk you to your car then, just in case.'

Sandy allowed herself a small sigh of relief. Finally, he seemed to have accepted her refusal.

'Just in case of what? In case I'm mugged between the door and my car?' she said sarcastically.

She needn't have bothered. Oliver ignored her remarks. Sandy compressed her mouth and stalked ahead of him. The man evidently had the hide of a rhinoceros. Nothing seemed able to penetrate it.

It was starting to snow again, she saw, as she practically erupted through the main entrance, such was her haste to get away from him. It was also icy underfoot. As soon as she discovered that, she slowed her pace and trod gingerly, but her caution was in vain. With no warning at all, her feet were sliding from beneath her and she felt herself begin to topple backwards. There was nothing she could do. She braced herself for the fall, but even as she had the thought, Oliver's arm shot out and he caught her in the nick of time.

'Steady, I've got you.'

And he had. It was only his powerful grip that saved her from an undignified and very painful tumble. In her relief, Sandy did what she'd vowed not to, and clung to him. Before she knew it, his arms were around her waist and they were facing each other, their heads only an inch apart.

'You have the most appealing mouth I've ever seen,' he murmured.

Sandy felt the blood racing through her veins, her pulses catapulted into overdrive. He had the trick of always doing the unexpected. Just when she believed she'd successfully steeled herself against him, she began to tremble.

'Come on, you're shivering,' Oliver remarked.

She wasn't the only one to be affected by their proximity. He'd also gone quite pale, Sandy noticed. What she should read into that, she didn't quite know.

He led her to her car, taking most of her weight upon himself, which was just as well because Sandy's feet were still sliding around on the treacherous, icy surface.

'Let's have your key,' he asked. 'I'll open the door.'

Sandy handed it over.

'In you get. Start it up. It's so cold this evening, it might be a bit sluggish.'

Sandy turned the key in the ignition. Nothing happened, apart from a couple of agonisingly slow turns, after which the engine died completely.

'Your battery's flat. It was probably already low and the extreme cold's finished it off.'

Sandy pulled the key back out and climbed from the car once more. She locked the door and, once again, began to pick her way across the carpark.

'Where on earth do you think you're going?' Oliver asked as he caught up with her.

'Home.'

'You can't walk in this weather and certainly not in those shoes. You'll never make it and it's starting to snow even harder.'

He was right, of course. Her feet were already unpleasantly wet and cold and she'd barely covered three feet of icy carpet. She also could hardly see across the carpark for driving snow. She knew she'd set herself an impossible task.

'Well, what else am I supposed to do?' she asked impatiently. 'I could go back inside and call a taxi, I suppose.'

'Don't be so stubborn. Let me drive you.'

As he spoke, Oliver was gently shepherding her towards his car. Sandy gave in. What would be the point in prolonging the argument? He was going to have his way, whatever she said or did.

Once they were inside his car, he passed her his mobile phone.

'Now, ring your mother. I insist on buying you a meal. It's my fault you're so late.'

Sandy did as he said. She was beginning to feel as if she'd been run over by a bulldozer. The man was indomitable. She wondered if he treated everyone like this, or if it was just her.

Felicity, her mother, not unexpectedly, was highly indignant.

'I've made you a meal. I suppose that man's at the bottom of this.'

As that man was sitting, listening unashamedly to her side of the conversation, Sandy could hardly confirm this.

'Keep it. I'll have it tomorrow.'

'For goodness' sake, Sandy, it'll be dried out and inedible. I'll bin it.'

'Please yourself,' Sandy agreed wearily. 'I'll see you later.'

Oliver took her to a local bistro, nothing too fancy, which was just as well, Sandy decided, as she was still wearing her working clothes. She seemed fated to dine with him in this state. The first thing he did was order a bottle of wine, the second was to pour Sandy a generous amount.

'You look as if you need this,' he said, after which he saluted her with his glass. 'Cheers, to us.'

She eyed him. That was a strange thing to say. What on earth could he mean? There was no 'us' as far as she was concerned. They ordered their food and Sandy discovered that she was starving, and soon was tucking in to a creamy chicken dish. Oliver watched her unobtrusively, a small smile playing about his mouth.

'It's a refreshing change to be with a woman who makes no pretence of enjoying her food. So many today are content to nibble upon a single leaf of lettuce and not much else.'

Was he referring to Portia? She certainly possessed a model-girl figure, in stark contrast to Sandy's. Was this his subtle way of telling her she was fat? In an instant, her appetite vanished and she laid down her fork.

'What's wrong?' Oliver asked.

'I've had enough. Don't want to pile on too many calories, after all.'

'Oh, you don't need to worry about that,' he assured her. 'You have an excellent figure.'

It could have been the effects of the wine on top of a hectic day but Sandy couldn't suppress a yawn.

'Sorry,' she mumbled from behind her hand. 'It's been a long day.'

'Yes, it has.'

Oliver smiled at her, almost tenderly. Yes, Sandy decided, the wine had definitely gone to her head. Either that or she was hallucinating, because the day Oliver smiled tenderly at her would be the day that someone proved the moon was indeed made of green cheese! Yet something strange was going on for all her scepticism. Firstly, he'd complimented her on her figure, then exhibited tenderness towards her. What was he up to?

'Come on, I'll take you home,' he was now offering.

Sandy stood up, only to almost fall to her knees. Oh, no! Too much wine after such a heavy day, it had to be, especially as she was unused to drinking so much.

No wonder she was reading things into Oliver's manner that weren't there.

She should have eaten her pride and swallowed more of her chicken. She smiled dreamily. Something sounded wrong about that. It should be swallowed pride and — oh, what the heck! It didn't matter. She sighed.

'Are you all right?'

'Just tired, that's all.'

She prayed he would believe her. She managed to make it in one piece to the car, mainly due once again to Oliver's supporting arm.

'We seem to be making a habit of this,' she stammered.

'I'm not complaining,' Oliver said quietly.

He seemed totally oblivious to her state, either that or he was used to women becoming intoxicated in his company. She squinted up at him, only to discover him staring down at her. She did manage to smile back.

The snow had lessened to just the odd, spiralling flake so it wasn't too hazardous a journey back to Sandy's house. The car did slide a couple of times but Oliver soon had it back under control again. At one point, Sandy found herself watching his hands upon the steering-wheel. The long fingers were firm, skilful, and suddenly, shockingly, she wondered what they would feel like upon her bare skin? It was what was needed to sober her up.

Once they were parked on the driveway, she turned to him and said, somewhat shakily, 'Thanks for the meal.'

He studied her for a long moment.

'It was the least I could do. I'll see you to the door.'

He swung round, preparing himself to climb out.

'No!' Sandy practically shouted the word. 'There's no need.'

How could she possibly tell him the real reason for her panic? He'd had his arms about her enough times today, and despite the amount she'd drunk, she knew she wouldn't be able to trust her self-control if he had to do it again.

Oliver, realising none of this, looked

taken aback, hurt even, by the vehemence of her response.

'OK. I'll wait here until you're inside then, if that's what you want.'

'I do. There's no need for both of us to get cold.'

But then, emboldened by the wine she'd consumed, and it could only have been that, she decided later, she turned and added impetuously, 'So, good-night, Oliver.'

She could see that she'd surprised him.

'Good-night, Sandy.'

She was acutely aware of his eyes upon her as she negotiated the snowy driveway. It warmed her, reassured her that if she should stumble and fall, he'd be there, at her side, instantly. She waited until she reached the door before she turned and waved. Only then did he drive away.

5

Sandy didn't see anything of Oliver after that for several days. Finally, he must have decided to leave the day-to-day business of Meredith's to its managerial staff. Had he concluded that they could be trusted, after all, or was it simply that he'd abandoned his efforts to win her over?

She should be glad about that, she told herself, so, why was it she felt so let down, so disappointed? She tried to convince herself it was because she couldn't see how she could justify calling herself his PA if she never saw him.

He did phone her a couple of times, the first time to ask her to e-mail the sets of figures he'd been so keen to have, the next to set out a workload that once again was heavy enough to keep her occupied for several days ahead. He did eventually show up at the office again.

'You see before you the new owner of Wilmsley Prior,' he told her. 'All signed and sealed as of a week ago, thanks to the good work of Portia and my solicitor.'

'Well, good for them,' Sandy murmured wryly.

So that's where he'd been, doing business with the lovely Portia. No wonder he hadn't had time to come to work. She wondered if all his other businesses had suffered from his neglect or if it was just Meredith's.

'I'm going to hold a housewarming party.'

She wondered why he was telling her.

'I will expect you to act as my hostess for the evening, in your capacity as my personal assistant, of course, nothing more.'

It was a second before she could speak, she was so shocked.

'Oh, of course. After all, what other capacity could I be there in?' she muttered.

He didn't seem to have recognised

her irony for what it was, or if he did, he chose to ignore it. He handed her a card, her invitation. She read it swiftly. The party was set for a fortnight's time.

'Maybe you could bring your mother and sister?' he asked.

'Well, I'll ask them but they're not really party people.'

Sandy couldn't think what else to say. She couldn't imagine her mother and sister consenting to attend any party thrown by Oliver Carlton, but she'd obviously have to go. Oliver had made it quite clear that it was to be regarded as part and parcel of her job, and with the high salary he was paying her, she could hardly refuse.

Every one of her expectations were fulfilled, with regards to her mother's and sister's reaction to Oliver's invitation.

'Go to Oliver Carlton's party?' Lucy shrieked. 'You have to be joking. I'd rather go to hell and back. And how you can ever consider being present?'

'It's my job to be there, Lucy,' Sandy told her.

'Huh! How many pieces of silver has he paid you, Judas?' Lucy spat out.

'You might enjoy it once you're there,' Sandy added. 'No expense will be spared, I'm sure.'

'I'm sure it won't, but the answer is still no, Sandy. Nothing, but nothing, would induce me to set foot in that man's house. At least when Dad gets back, I'll be able to say honestly, I stayed loyal to him.'

Felicity seemed considerably less hostile to the idea.

'It would be nice. I haven't been to a party in ages.'

'You can't go.' Lucy was outraged. 'Not after what he did to Dad. What's wrong with you two? Does integrity mean nothing?'

'No, you're right,' Felicity agreed, a little wistfully it had to be said. 'It wouldn't be the done thing.'

And that was that. Sandy had to admit to relief. Despite issuing the invitation, she'd been in dread of what either her mother, or much more likely, her sister would come out with to Oliver, in the event that they accepted his invitation. Lucy had never been one to pull her punches.

It was her mother, however, whom Sandy was mainly concerned about. Felicity had been behaving strangely now for over a week, taking several brief but mysterious phone calls, each one no more than a couple of seconds in length, only to go out immediately afterwards. Sandy had quizzed her about them, to no avail.

'Oh, it's just a friend,' Felicity would say absentmindedly. 'She rings when she wants some company. Her husband is away a lot at the moment, on business.'

'What friend?'

'Joan Hamley.'

Sandy knew Joan. She'd been a friend of her mother's for years, so she thought no more about it, until she'd bumped into Joan in the newsagent's.

'Hello, Joan,' she'd said. 'Did you and Mum have a good time last night?'

Felicity had once again rushed to the phone when it rang before poking her head around the lounge door to say, 'I'm off to Joan's. See you later.'

Sandy had been glad she was going out again, even if it was just to a friend's house. It had certainly cheered Felicity up. She'd even started to sing again as she performed her household chores. She hadn't done that since her husband had disappeared.

But Joan had looked visibly uncomfortable as she'd said, 'Oh, yes, the usual, you know.'

Then she'd swung back to the sales assistant, paid for her paper and almost run from the shop. Sandy had stared after her in bewilderment. What on earth was all that about? She'd looked embarrassed. She certainly had wanted to get away before Sandy could ask any more questions. Sandy had walked from the shop, her brow creased in a puzzled frown. Things no longer looked as clear-cut as her mother had made out. The pair of them were hiding something, she'd decided later. But what?

The day before the party, Oliver spoke to Sandy.

'Could you come to the house tomorrow, around mid-afternoon,' he asked. 'It's just so that you can be there to supervise the caterers. I have to be out, a business appointment, otherwise I'd do it, although I do think a woman has a better eye for that sort of thing. Bring your evening clothes. You can use one of the bedrooms to change in. Oh, by the way, are your mother and sister coming?'

'Um — I meant to tell you, actually, but I haven't seen much of you. They're both otherwise engaged, I'm afraid.'

Oliver gave her a level look.

'That's a shame. I was looking forward to meeting them.'

He didn't believe her. Sandy knew that as surely as if he'd said so. She'd never been a good liar. Even as a girl, her mother had always been able to see straight through her.

Sandy turned up at the house promptly at three-thirty the next day. June had been intrigued when she'd said where she was going.

'Fancy inviting you, not that there's any reason why he shouldn't,' she'd put in hastily. 'It's just that I'd have thought he'd have kept it to his posh friends.'

'Oh, I'm not a guest as such,' Sandy told her. 'I'm there in the capacity of his PA.'

'Really,' June had murmured, giving Sandy a decidedly sly look. 'If you ask me, I think he fancies you.'

'Don't be ridiculous, June.'

Sandy's retort was sharp, mainly due to embarrassment.

'I've seen the way he looks at you when he's here, and it's not the way the boss usually regards his PA, believe me. I think you're in with a chance.'

Sandy snorted.

'A chance at what? Being on the butt end of his moods and orders? That I can do without, thank you very much.'

But June's words had given her much

food for thought. Oliver did seem to single her out for his attention; when he was in the office, which wasn't that often. But surely that could be put down to the fact that she was supposed to be his personal assistant. However, if June had noticed and speculated about it, how many others had done the same? And now, he'd asked her to be his hostess for the evening, something she would have deemed well outside the boundaries of her normal duties as his assistant.

People were going to start to talk if she knew the good folk of Wilmsley, because several of them were going to be at the party, Mrs Ripley for one, Oliver's nearest neighbour and an inveterate gossip. If she glimpsed a sign of any partiality on Oliver's part for Sandy, it would soon be all round the town and then her mother would hear and so would Lucy. Then the sparks would really fly. She'd have to try to keep her distance from him, even if it meant appearing a little rude.

There wasn't much for her to do when she got to Wilmsley Prior. The caterers and party organisers had everything in hand. She couldn't imagine why Oliver had wanted her to be here. Knowing him as she was beginning to, he wouldn't have hired them if he hadn't been confident of their ability. As it was, she felt completely superfluous, in the way, even, she decided.

Eventually, in an effort to look busy, she volunteered to arrange the flowers. They'd already been picked so all she had to do was place them attractively in large vases and then distribute them around the house. Doing this gave her the opportunity to view all that Oliver had had done.

The changes were subtle but they were there — fresher décor; luxurious curtains, swagged and draped; antique furniture and carpets, all in keeping with the period of the house. Everything was of the best possible quality without being overtly showy.

All in all, he'd kept his word and skilfully retained the charm and character of the place. It was truly marvellous what having money could do, and in so short a time! No doubt, he'd employed teams of people to do everything for him. She wondered how closely Portia Hollis had been involved.

Half an hour before the guests were expected to arrive, Sandy went to the bedroom that she'd been shown to by the woman who'd informed her she was Oliver's recently-appointed housekeeper. Once again, Sandy wondered why he'd wanted her to be here when he had domestic staff who could have supervised arrangements far more capably than she had done. She was pleased to see that there was a luxurious en-suite bathroom so she could treat herself to a hot shower before dressing.

She was slipping her silk top over her head when she heard the sounds of a car arriving. She ran to the window and peeped out from behind the curtain. It was Oliver. He strode into the house and moments later she heard him go past her door, presumably on his way to his own room.

She took another look in the cheval mirror, tweaked her hair until it was just right, sprayed on her favourite perfume, and then, eventually, went out and downstairs. Oliver came up behind her.

'Very nice,' he murmured, appraising her sage green silk tunic and black evening trousers. 'That green's definitely your colour. Can I tempt you to a glass of champagne before everyone starts arriving?'

People seemed to drift in for hours. He must have invited at least one hundred or so, maybe more. Oliver had insisted she stand at his side to greet them, which was exactly what Sandy hadn't wanted to do. It seemed to bestow a significance upon her presence that she'd been keen to avoid.

Mrs Ripley, just as she had expected, had commented upon this.

'Why, Miss Owen, I hadn't expected

to see you here, not like this.'

She'd then sneaked a sideways look at Oliver who'd returned the glance with a self-assured smile.

'Miss Owen is acting as my hostess for the evening,' he'd told her.

Miss Ripley regarded Sandy with interest.

'Really? Are your mother and sister here, too, my dear?'

'Um — no, they couldn't make it.'

She hated having to lie.

'Well, I would have thought they'd make the effort for a do like this, especially with you being the hostess. Oh, well, it's none of my business.'

'No,' Sandy murmured beneath her breath.

She didn't think anyone would have heard but Oliver must have, because she felt his gaze lingering, with warm amusement, upon her.

'It's more than time that your mother started going out again in my opinion. She can't shut herself away for ever. No man's worth that,' the woman persisted and she gave Oliver the sort of look that suggested he was solely to blame for Felicity's absence from the celebrations, which was far too close to the truth for Sandy's peace of mind.

It was almost as if Miss Ripley knew what had happened. But she couldn't do, could she? The Owen family had kept everything very much to themselves. In fact, Oliver Carlton's name had never been mentioned in connection with her father's redundancy and subsequent problems. All people knew, apart from their very closest friends, who certainly wouldn't have said anything to anyone, was that Martin had left to start a new life for them all in Spain and was still there.

'No, Miss Ripley.'

Sandy, acutely aware of Oliver's curious glance still upon her, swung to greet the next guest, who just happened to be Portia Hollis. This was getting better and better.

'Have you heard from your father lately?' Portia asked pointedly, her gaze glittering with what looked like spite to Sandy.

Did she think that Oliver should have asked her to be his hostess for the evening rather than her, Sandy? It would seem likely, judging by that expression in her eyes.

'His last known whereabouts was somewhere in Spain, wasn't it? All very odd, almost as if he were running from something, or someone.'

Sandy felt the colour rising in her face.

'Yes, he's still there,' she mumbled.

'And you and your family haven't joined him yet? I'm surprised, I must say, especially after selling your home. Although, of course, you didn't make a great deal on it, certainly not enough to set you all up over there. Still, you must miss him.'

In sheer desperation, Sandy turned to Oliver, who'd been listening to all of this with a frankly puzzled frown upon his face.

'Would you excuse me for a few

moments? I need to go to the — '

'Yes, of course.'

He looked concerned and June's words that he fancied her returned to her.

'Are you OK? You look a little feverish,' he went on and he put out a hand as if to touch her forehead.

Sandy jerked away before he could do so. Goodness knows what construction people like Miss Ripley would place upon such an intimate gesture.

'I'm fine, just a headache. Excuse me,' she said and turned and fled.

'Oh, dear,' she heard Portia saying with false concern. 'Was it something I said? I didn't mean to upset her.'

Sandy didn't wait to hear what Oliver replied to that. She all but ran to the cloakroom, where she locked herself in one of the cubicles.

She had to come out of the cloakroom eventually, of course, as much as she would have loved to stay there. By the time she did, all of the guests had arrived so she had, at least, avoided having to greet any more of them at Oliver's side. That should have pleased Portia, as must the fact that she was currently being held, rather too closely, in her host's arms as they danced.

'Now, there's a surprise,' Sandy muttered sardonically to herself.

She walked to the bar and asked for a glass of white wine. Maybe it would lift her mood a little. It didn't, mainly because Oliver ignored her, dancing with virtually every woman in the room except her.

The thought came to her fleetingly that he was punishing her in some way for deserting him as she had done. She did dance, of course. There were plenty of other men available as partners, but somehow, they didn't make up for Oliver's neglect. Why she should be so bothered she didn't know, as he'd made clear in the first place, she was only here in her rôle as his PA and she herself had vowed to keep her distance, at all times. She'd done her duty in, firstly, overseeing the preparations, and then standing at his side greeting his guests. She supposed she could legitimately leave now. She was about to go and fetch her coat and do just that when Oliver appeared before her.

'My turn now.'

He smiled, tantalisingly, at her, his glittering, tawny gaze lingering almost sensuously upon the rosy flush of her cheeks.

'Come and dance with me, Sandy.'

She was tempted to tell him to go, but she didn't, mainly because she needed to keep her job, at least, that's what she told herself. However, she had almost immediate cause to regret her compliance because as he took her in his arms, the music disconcertingly changed from a heavy rock number to a smoochy waltz. It was the last thing she had expected.

She glanced up at him, uncertainly. Would he still wish to dance with her? For a fleeting moment, Sandy wondered if he'd had something to do with the choice of music, but he was probably as embarrassed as she was, just making a better job of concealing it.

But when he subsequently pulled her closer, Sandy found herself wondering all over again, especially when she glanced up at him, for the second time in as many minutes, and encountered his gleaming, fathomless gaze. To her intense shame, and despite all her admonitions to herself, she felt herself once again responding to his nearness. She simply couldn't help it. She gave a slight shiver. It had been a while since she'd been held in such an intimate manner, and Oliver Carlton was the very last man she should be feeling this overwhelming desire for.

When he lowered his head to let it rest against hers and then nestled his lips into her hair, she wondered if he could be tipsy. It seemed the only possible explanation, yet he hadn't looked intoxicated.

'Sandy,' he murmured unexpectedly,

'thank you for all you've done.'

He lifted his head and looked down at her, something that closely resembled desire glittering in his eyes.

'Every man here is envying me, not surprisingly. You look lovely.'

Sandy tore herself free. She couldn't let this go on. It was too dangerous. Any moment now, she'd be responding and that would be the ultimate betrayal, of her father, of her family, of her own self-respect.

'I'm sorry, I have to go. You don't need me any longer.'

She turned away, but not before she'd noted the expression upon Oliver's face. He'd looked completely taken aback, and totally sober. He caught hold of her arm and swung her to face him. His hand was as steady as a rock upon her skin. He clearly wasn't anything like as affected as she had been by the closeness of their dancing.

'What is it?' he asked quietly. 'What's wrong?'

'Nothing. It's just, I'm tired. It's been

a long day. So if you don't need me any longer — '

'But I do. Sandy!'

'Oliver!'

It was Portia, and she was staring bitterly, accusingly at Sandy.

'I've been waiting for another dance. You said you would when you'd done your duty rounds.'

So, dancing with his personal assistant had been nothing more than his duty. The pain of rejection shot through her. Well, that did it. There was nothing like a dose of brutal truth to bring one back down to earth. How could she possibly have thought she detected desire in his glance, even for as much as a second? He wasn't interested in her, other than to exploit her usefulness.

'He's all yours, Portia,' she managed to say. 'I've got to go.'

'Just a second, Portia,' Oliver spat out and swung back to Sandy again. 'Sandy, I know there's something wrong.'

But he was too late. Sandy had seized her chance and made her escape. She retrieved her coat quickly and fled — away from temptation, and more importantly, away from the man she was in deadly danger of beginning to fall in love with.

Sandy let herself into the house quietly. She didn't even switch on the hall light. She didn't want to wake her mother and Lucy. She couldn't face any more of the sort of recriminations she'd been subjected to when she'd first told them of Oliver's party and her rôle with regards to it. She just wanted to get to bed, to go to sleep, and thus banish the whole disastrous evening from her thoughts. She wished now she'd listened to them and told Oliver she couldn't do it. But how could she have done that when she was supposed to be his PA, although, in all honesty, she hadn't expected the job to include hosting his private parties.

She was walking quietly towards the stairs, intent on getting to her bedroom as quickly as she could, when a muffled giggle reached her ears. She stood still and listened. That was Lucy. What was she doing still up? Sandy glanced at the hall clock. It was only eleven o'clock. She'd go and say hello, or rather good-night. Her sister was probably watching a film on television.

As she reached out for the door handle to the sitting-room, another laugh sounded, a man's laugh. Sandy froze for a second but then instinct took over and she threw the door open. Lucy sprang up from the settee, her expression one of almost comical dismay. She didn't look too steady on her feet either.

'Why, Sandy, I wasn't expecting you yet.'

Sandy looked from her sister to the person who sprawled in one of the two armchairs, a tattooed, earring-festooned young man.

'Obviously not,' she said.

'This is Damian, a mate of mine from college,' Lucy said rather guiltily.

'Hello,' Sandy replied and looked back at her sister. 'Where's Mum?'

Lucy shrugged, almost insolently.

'How would I know? She went out.'

'So, what's going on here then?'

Sandy glanced back at the boy. He didn't look much older than Lucy. His eyes were closed, as if he were bored with the whole thing. Sandy frowned.

'We're just having fun, you know, like you've been doing tonight.'

'I would hardly describe what I've been doing as fun,' Sandy retorted sharply. 'It was part of my job.'

Damian's eyes snapped open.

'Wh — what sort of job's that then?'

His words were slurred, Sandy noticed, and a horrible suspicion took hold of her. She looked back at Lucy. The younger girl's eyes were dark, glittering.

'Have you been drinking, Lucy?'

She glanced around the room. There were a couple of empty glasses and several discarded drink cans.

'So, what if I have? It was only lager.'

She began to giggle, dropping back down on to the settee again as she did so, before dissolving into gales of laughter.

'Only lager! You're drunk, Lucy.'

Sandy's voice sharpened.

'Just a little bit.'

'I think you're more than a little bit drunk, Lucy.'

She turned to Damian. Of the two of them, he looked the most sober.

'How many has she had?'

'I dunno. Three or four.'

'And you brought the cans with you, presumably?'

'Yeah.'

'Get out.'

'Don't worry, I was just goin' anyway. No fun with big sister here.'

He slid his arms into a grubby blue denim jacket.

'See you, Luce.'

Once they were alone again, Sandy turned on her sister.

'How could you be so stupid?'

'Stupid? Like you, you mean? Going to that party? If that's not stupid, when you think what that man's done to us.'

The front door opened.

'Hi, I'm home,' their mum called.

'In here,' Sandy called back.

'Why, you're back?' Felicity said in surprise. 'Party no good then?'

'I was tired. Where have you been, Mum?'

'At Jean's, where I usually am when I'm out. We had a take-away.'

She smiled at her younger daughter.

'Did your friend come, darling?'

'You knew he was coming?' Sandy cried.

Felicity appeared surprised once more.

'Yes, of course. I was glad that Lucy would have some company with the both of us out.'

'Have you met this friend?'

'Why, no. Lucy said it was one of her college friends. I couldn't see any harm in it.'

'They've been drinking,' Sandy burst out.

Felicity's eyes widened.

'Lucy? Is this true?'

'So what?'

Lucy was the picture of insolence.

'You were both out enjoying yourselves, so why shouldn't I do the same?'

'Oh, darling, whatever would your father say?'

'I have no idea but as he isn't here to say anything, it doesn't really matter, does it? And now, I'm going to bed.'

She got up from the settee and, with her head high, began to walk towards the door. If she meant to make a dignified exit, it fell far short of that. She tripped over the corner of a rug and fell flat.

'Blast!' she cried.

'Oh, Lucy,' her mother said, running across to her.

'Leave me.'

Lucy put out a hand, warning her mother not to come any closer. Sandy could take no more.

'Go to bed, Lucy, and we'll talk about this tomorrow.'

'Oh, no, we won't. You're not my mother. Just keep your nose out. In fact, both of you can keep your noses out. It's my life and I'll do what I want with it.'

Next morning, they discovered that Lucy had meant what she'd said. She'd gone, taking a fair bit of what she possessed with her. Felicity was distraught.

'This is my fault. I should have checked who she was seeing. Do you think she's gone off with this — this boy?'

'Damian. I don't know. I hope not. He didn't seem a very good influence. I'll ring some of her friends, see if she's with them. She can't have gone far.'

But nobody had seen Lucy or knew where she was.

'Go and look for her, Sandy, please,' Felicity pleaded. 'You hear of young girls sleeping rough. It's so cold and she's not got much money. Anything could happen to her, anything at all.'

As it was Saturday and she didn't have to be at work, Sandy did as her mother suggested, knowing in her heart of hearts that it was a fruitless exercise. If Lucy really wanted to scare them, and Sandy was growing more and more convinced that that was what was at the bottom of this, Lucy wouldn't stay where she could be found quickly.

Sandy was right. There was no sign of her sister, anywhere. Sandy wanted to ring the police but Felicity stopped her.

'Leave it, just for a day or two. She might come home of her own accord. We don't want the police involved, not until they have to be.'

Sunday came and went without any sign of Lucy, but Felicity was still adamant she didn't want the police called.

'She'll come back,' she kept saying, 'once she gets hungry and cold. I know she will. She'd never leave home for good.'

She seemed positive of this, and even went out at one point, to see Jean.

'Mother,' Sandy had said, 'you need to be here in case there's any news.'

She'd asked all of Lucy's friends to

keep their eyes and ears open for sightings of Lucy and to ring them instantly if she was spotted.

'I won't be long. I just need to talk to Jean.'

Sandy went to work on Monday morning because she couldn't think of anything else to do. In any case, she needed to see Oliver if he turned up, to make some sort of excuse for her premature departure from his party on Friday evening.

She'd been extremely rude, she'd decided in retrospect, and some sort of apology needed to be made. Of course, whether he'd accept it remained to be seen. He might well simply sack her. She groaned to herself. That would be all she needed. To lose her job and her sister all in a matter of days.

'Stay by the phone, Mother,' she said before she left, 'and if you hear anything, ring me at work and I'll come straight home.'

'Good grief, you look terrible,' June said, by way of a greeting at the office.

'Is it the flu? There's a lot of it about. Or are you still hung over from Friday evening? How did the party go, by the way?'

Sandy smiled weakly. She'd decided not to say anything at work about Lucy's disappearance, not yet anyway. She and Felicity were still hoping Lucy would return home within the next day or two.

'Oh, it went well. I left early. I wasn't feeling too good, so maybe it is a touch of the flu. I hadn't considered that.'

She smiled weakly for a second time and settled down to work.

Oliver turned up half an hour later. He took one look at her face and shadowed eyes and commanded, 'My office, now.'

6

Sandy got to her feet, somewhat shakily it had to be said. Oliver looked frighteningly grim. He obviously hadn't forgiven her for her abrupt departure from the party on Friday.

She followed him into his office, where he waved her into the chair that faced his desk. For his part, he remained standing in front of it, his arms crossed over his chest. Sandy immediately felt intimidated. She wondered if that was deliberate. He loomed over her.

'OK, what's wrong? And don't say nothing because I won't believe you.'

To Sandy's horror, she felt a stinging behind the lids of her eyes. She couldn't cry, not here, not in front of him!

'Sandy, tell me, right now.'

It was the last straw for Sandy. She couldn't help it. A single tear spilled and ran down on her cheek. Furious with herself, she dashed it away, and then, in the next second, heard herself telling him everything. She couldn't believe it. She held nothing back. She told him all about Lucy and Damian and the drinking, about the ensuing row, about getting up the following morning only to find her sister gone.

'I should have talked to her Friday night instead of going to bed,' she agonised. 'It's all my fault.'

Oliver didn't say anything for a long moment.

'You mustn't blame yourself but, well, why didn't you?'

'I was tired. I didn't feel that well.'

'Was that why you left the party early?'

His voice was low and intense, his gaze watchful.

'Yes.'

It seemed much the easier thing to agree with him. She could hardly tell him she'd left because of what Portia had said, about their dance being merely a duty for him. It all seemed unimportant now anyway, in the light of Lucy's disappearance.

'Have you rung the police?'

'No. Mother and I are hoping she'll come back of her own accord. I mean, we know she hasn't been abducted or anything like that. She simply packed her bags and left. They probably wouldn't do anything anyway. Thousands of young people go missing of their own free will each year, or so I've read.'

'Still, they could keep their eyes open for her.'

'Yes, you're right. I'll ring them tomorrow. Give her one more night.'

She wrapped both arms around herself and shrank down farther into the chair. She looked vulnerable and utterly defenceless. Oliver hesitated for a moment and then he leaned forward and pulled her out of the chair and into his arms.

'I'm sure it will be all right. She'll come home, Sandy. Most do, apparently, when they get hungry.'

His gentle kindness was the last straw. She'd been expecting the sack and here he was, comforting her instead. The stress, the anxiety, the lack of sleep, the sheer misery of the past forty-eight hours, all combined to overwhelm her. She began to sob, uncontrollably, helplessly, her body shuddering against his, her arms going round him for support.

To his credit, he didn't make any move to pull away. In fact, he drew her closer if anything. It felt right, so secure. She could have stayed like that for evermore but knew that she couldn't. Lord knows what he was thinking of her as it was. Gently, she freed herself and took a step back, putting a safe distance between them once more.

'I'm sorry.'

'I'm not.'

She didn't quite know what to make of that quiet remark. Once again, she found herself questioning if June could be right about him. He certainly hadn't seemed at all put out by her falling into his embrace. He had seemed to welcome it, in fact. He was smiling now and proffering a handkerchief.

'Be my guest.'

Gratefully, Sandy took it, mopped away her tears and blew her nose. She had to be wrong; June had to be wrong. There was no sign of anything more than friendliness upon his face. Mind you, she hadn't been able to see his expression whilst she'd been in his arms. Maybe that would have revealed something.

'Thank you,' she mumbled. 'I'll wash it and return it.'

'No need. I've plenty more where that came from.'

'Right, I'll get back to work then.'

She turned towards the door.

'Sandy.'

'Yes?'

'Let me know when your sister returns, will you?'

That evening when Sandy arrived home, it was to find Lucy there, sitting in the lounge with Felicity, sadly, a still defiant and openly rebellious Lucy.

'I ran out of money, that's the only reason I'm back.'

She scowled at her elder sister.

'Lucy, running away from home is not the answer. You're only seventeen,' Sandy began.

'Yes, all right, Sandy,' Felicity put in. 'She's back, that's the main thing and she's promised not to do such a thing again, haven't you, darling?'

'Yes, well, for now. But I'm not having her telling me what to do or not to do.'

Lucy jabbed a defiant finger at Sandy.

'OK, Lucy,' Sandy agreed, lifting two hands into the air in surrender. 'But please be careful about whom you mix with.'

'Who I mix with? What about who you mix with? The man who drove our father to attempt suicide! You're always on at me,' Lucy raged. 'Mum, will you speak to her?'

'Sandy, dear, it's all right. Lucy and I have an understanding.'

'Oh, really, what sort of understanding?' Sandy bit out, more than a little hurt that she'd been excluded from this conversation. 'The understanding that she does what she likes and you say nothing?'

Lucy leaped up from the settee.

'There's no talking to you, is there?' she exclaimed, and flounced from the room. 'I'm going upstairs. I have work to do.'

'Lucy,' Sandy called after her, 'I'm sorry. That was harsh of me.'

'Oh, Sandy,' Felicity said, somewhat irritably. 'Just leave her to me. She really has promised that she won't do such a thing again.'

'I'm sorry. Blame it on a bad day at work.'

But from then on, unfortunately, things went from bad to worse. Out of the blue, an old flame reappeared in Sandy's life — Jon Deakin.

He was waiting at the house when

she arrived home the following after-noon and Lucy was with him. Sandy sighed to herself when she saw him. This was all she needed. Her relation-ship with him had been a disaster.

'Jon,' she said. 'I thought . . . ' and she almost added, 'you'd gone for good.'

'I never intended to stay away. The folks have been nagging me to come home, so I have.'

He hesitated for a moment.

'Actually, I came to tell you that I've managed to get a job at Carrington's. I thought you should know.'

That startled Sandy. Carrington's was one of Meredith's main competi-tors.

'I have to say,' he went on with a grim smile, 'I had hoped for a warmer welcome from you.'

'Had you?' she asked coolly.

'Isn't it wonderful that he's back?' Lucy put in breathlessly.

She'd been gazing at Jon, her heart in her eyes for anyone to see. Sandy remembered then that Lucy had had a crush on Jon for as long as he and Sandy had gone out together. His sudden departure for the south east and a better job had devastated her, put an end to her girlish hopes that one day, when she was older he'd turn to her. At the time, she'd blamed Sandy for his leaving.

'It's all your fault,' she'd raged, tearfully. 'You've never treated him right. Now he's gone and who knows when we'll see him again.'

'Never, if we're in luck,' Sandy had quipped. 'Lucy, you don't know him like I do.'

'No, and now I never will, thanks to you.'

Lucy had retreated to her bedroom at the time where she'd stayed until the following day, refusing to speak to anyone, refusing to eat, even. Now, the last thing Sandy wanted was to see her younger sister get involved with him. At thirty-one, Jon was too old for a seventeen-year-old and far too worldly wise.

She wondered if he'd deliberately

applied for the post at Carrington's knowing they were Meredith's main competitor in the engineering and manufacturing field. She wouldn't put it past him. She'd always suspected that Jon was the possessor of a vindictive streak, although, she had to admit, it hadn't revealed itself until the end of their relationship.

Unexpectedly, he smiled, but not at her. He was looking at Lucy, even though he was speaking to Sandy.

'I know we'll be competitors but that needn't affect our friendship, need it?'

Sandy, once again, felt a sharp stab of unease. She had to do something, as reluctant as she was to spend any more time with him than she had to.

'Lucy,' she said, 'could you give us a minute? I'd like to have a private word with Jon.'

Glaring indignantly at her sister, Lucy flounced from the room.

'I'll see you, will I, Jon?' she asked before she'd gone.

Her expression was pathetically eager.

Sandy's heart lurched at the sight. Lucy was at such an impressionable age. Someone like Jon could so easily turn her head, hurt her. He'd threatened her, after all, Sandy recalled, before he'd left.

'You'll pay for this, my girl. No-one, but no-one, turns me down.'

He'd been filled with bitterness and something more, something that had filled Sandy with misgiving. She'd told herself that it was all talk. Jon wouldn't really try to hurt her. Now, looking at him again, she wasn't so sure that he wouldn't be above using Lucy to get at Sandy.

' 'Course you will, babe,' he answered Lucy.

Sandy turned to him once her sister was gone, all semblance of politeness gone.

'Stay away from Lucy. She's only eighteen. Too young to cope with you and your games.'

Jon looked wounded. Anyone but Sandy would have been completely taken in.

'What games?'

'The games you played with me, or rather with other women.'

'Oh, those. Well, if you'd been a bit more forthcoming, I wouldn't have had to look elsewhere. It was your own fault.'

'My fault? You knew I wanted to wait until we were married for our relationship to become intimate. If you couldn't respect my feelings, well, the fact is I could never have trusted you again. Lucy can't trust you now. I don't want to see her hurt as I was. But it wasn't just your infidelity, Jon. It was the way you reacted when I found you out. You became extremely abusive.'

'Oh, for goodness' sake!'

He regarded her contemptuously.

'Tell me, Sandy, are you still so detached? Or has this new boss of yours broken your defences? I hear he's pretty hot stuff and not just in the business department. His ability to seduce women is pretty much legendary.'

'Get out,' she said, 'and stay away from Lucy.'

From then on, things went from bad to worse for Sandy, at home as well as at work.

Lucy wasn't speaking to her. She'd discovered that Sandy had warned Jon off and that could only have come from Jon himself, Sandy concluded. Felicity was remote, too, and preoccupied. She was still getting the phone calls a couple of times a week and going out immediately afterwards, once more arousing Sandy's suspicions as to what was going on with her and Joan, making her wonder if everything was as simple and above board as Felicity was making out.

Then, just to add to all of this, Oliver informed her that he wanted to attend a trade exhibition in Birmingham.

'We'll go on Monday.'

'We?' she echoed.

'Well, naturally. I'll expect you as my PA to come with me. Is that a problem? Things are back to normal at home, aren't they?'

She had, as he had requested, told

him of Lucy's return. He'd looked almost as relieved as Sandy had felt.

'I told you she'd come back,' had been his instant response. 'Is everything OK now?'

'Yes. My mother and Lucy have reached an understanding,' she'd told him.

'Well, that's good, isn't it?'

'I hope so. I certainly hope so.'

Now, when Sandy didn't answer him immediately, he said, 'Sandy?'

'Oh, yes, everything's fine.'

But the truth was, she wasn't at all sure of that, and when all was said and done, she did feel that she shouldn't be away from home, not just at the moment. Still, just a day away wouldn't hurt, she was sure. Nothing could go wrong in that short a time.

'Good. We'll stay two days, that should be long enough.'

'Two days!' she exclaimed in dismay. 'Is that necessary?'

'I think so. It's a large exhibition. As it is, we'll be pushed to see everything we need to. Now, can you make hotel reservations for the Monday night? As near to the exhibition centre as you can, and I'll pick you up at your house that morning. Seven-thirty, sharp.'

As much as she felt like pleading for a shorter visit, she could see it would be useless. She sighed and picked up the phone to make the hotel booking. After her fifth try she knew they had a problem. Everywhere was fully booked. Maybe she should give up. That way they couldn't stay overnight. They'd have to make do with just a day. But her conscience wouldn't allow her to do that and, finally, on her seventh attempt, she found a hotel that had had a couple of cancellations.

On the Monday morning, as commanded, Sandy was ready on the dot of seven-thirty. Two minutes after, precisely, Oliver's car pulled up in front of the house. It was a miserable morning of sleety rain and a biting, northeasterly wind. She ran to the car, where Oliver stood with the passenger door open.

'You needn't have got out,' she said as she climbed inside.

'I always get out for my passengers,' he said. 'Why should you be an exception?'

Sandy had no answer for that as Oliver walked around the car and got into the driver's seat.

'Is it warm enough for you?'

'It's gorgeous,' she told him, relaxing back into the seat and loosening her coat and scarf.

He eyed her keenly.

'Everything all right in there?'

'At the moment.'

She frowned as she thought about her sister and Jon. Lucy, as well as her mother, had been out on the last two evenings. Lucy, when Sandy had quizzed her, had unbent enough to say she was going to see a college friend but as she hadn't seemed able to look Sandy in the eye, Sandy had come to the conclusion that she was lying. She was meeting Jon.

Sandy didn't know what to do about

it. If she actively tried to stop Lucy seeing Jon, she was sure it would only make her all the more keen.

Sandy decided to confide in Oliver. He'd been very understanding before when she'd cried on his shoulder and she did desperately need to confide in some-one.

'An old friend of mine turned up the other day,' she began.

Oliver, of course, instantly picked up on her hesitation.

'Friend? You sound doubtful about that.'

'Well, an old boyfriend, actually.'

He swivelled in his seat and subjected her to a particularly penetrating stare.

'And?'

'I wasn't pleased to see him. We parted under less than happy circumstances.'

He didn't speak, simply waited for her to go on. His jaw had noticeably hardened, though, and his mouth had thinned, as if he wasn't best pleased at what she was saying.

'We rowed and I finished with him.

He was angry, to say the least.'

'So why's he back now? Is he pestering you? Because if he is — '

'He isn't. Well, at least, not me.'

'What do you mean?'

'He's making moves on Lucy.'

Oliver's gaze narrowed, became even more penetrating than it already was.

'And you don't like that?'

He was making it sound as if she were jealous and it wasn't that way at all.

'No, I don't,' she cried. 'For a start, he's a good bit older than her.'

She was determined to disabuse Oliver of the notion that she was in any way peeved by Lucy maybe having snatched what she'd given up.

'How much older?'

'Fourteen years.'

'That is a bit old for a seventeen year old.'

'A bit? It's way too old.'

'Are you sure that's all that's bothering you?'

'No,' she snapped. 'He's also a very bad influence.'

'In what way?'

'Oh, all sorts of ways. He's a very manipulative man and I don't trust him.'

'Have you told Lucy all of this?'

'Oh, yes. She refused to listen. In fact, I think she's been meeting him secretly, although when I asked her who she was going out to see, she said a college friend.'

'Maybe she was telling the truth.'

'I don't think so. There was something about the way she wouldn't look me in the eye.'

'Well, give it time,' he said. 'I'm sure she'll see through him, the same as you did. The more you oppose her, the keener she'll get.'

As that was the conclusion Sandy herself had reached, she didn't feel the need to say anything else on the subject. The journey passed easily, as they discussed the people they intended to see at the exhibition and formulated their plans for the two days.

Almost before she knew it, they were

parking in one of the massive car parks that surrounded the national exhibition centre. A bus took them to the halls that housed the exhibits and almost at once they were thrust into the hurly-burly of the busy exhibition.

The day passed like lightning and by six o'clock they were both showing signs of tiredness.

'I think we've done enough for one day,' Oliver assured her. 'Let's go to the hotel. I could murder a gin and tonic. How about you?'

She smiled at him.

'It's been a good day,' he continued. 'Thank you for all your help. We've got ourselves several potential customers amongst the people we've talked to as well as a few good sources for the component parts that we need. It goes without saying, I couldn't have done it without your input.'

Sandy was flattered by this, as well as puzzled. Oliver Carlton wasn't turning out to be anything like the sort of tyrannical go-getter as rumour painted him. And certainly not the sort of man to sack a loyal employee at a moment's notice. She eyed him.

For all that he said he was tired, there was still a dynamism about him, which made her suspect that it was mainly for her sake that he was calling it a day. She was exhausted and she knew, from past experience, that her face would be showing it. The colour had a habit of draining from her skin, and as if that weren't revealing enough, dark shadows would appear beneath her eyes.

Nonetheless, she was grateful for his consideration. Once again, it contrasted with her original concept of him. The tyrant she had believe him to be would have kept her going for as long as he saw fit.

It was instantly obvious to Sandy that the hotel, when they reached it, was far from being the height of luxury that she was sure her employer was accustomed to. The outside was shabby and sorely in need of some care. Sandy felt a stab of anxiety. She hoped the inside would be better. If it wasn't, goodness knows what Oliver would think. He'd probably demand that they go somewhere else.

However, other than a narrowed glance at the peeling paintwork, Oliver gave no other indication that he was less than satisfied with what she had booked. Fortunately, the inside was a distinct improvement on the exterior so Sandy felt able to relax again. Just to be on the safe side, though, while Oliver checked them in, she indulged herself in a swift look around.

She was pleasantly reassured by the fact that although the reception area was small, it was spotlessly clean and very comfortable looking. She found a small bar through an archway, again with comfortable seating, and a glass door that led into a fair-sized dining-room. A second door led into a more than adequate sitting-room.

'Right,' Oliver said as he joined her, a grin on his face, 'had a good look round?'

He'd clearly noticed her opening doors

to have a look inside. She nodded, feeling more than a little foolish and very juvenile. He'd probably think she never stayed in hotels, which, in all honesty, she didn't, very often. She didn't want him to know that, however. He'd most likely have her down as a small-town unsophisticate, which, of course, once again, she was.

'So,' he murmured, 'if it all passes muster, lead me to the bar.'

Sandy hesitated. She felt slightly grubby and decidedly creased and she was sure that tiredness had etched lines as well as shadows upon her face, She wasn't normally a vain person but the idea of sitting opposite Oliver and being subjected to that penetrating gaze of his was suddenly more than she could bear.

'Um, would you mind if I said no to a drink? What I really want is a bath first.'

Oliver regarded her in silence for a moment or two, then said, 'Yes, you do look tired.'

So, she'd been right. He had noticed

her pallor and dark shadows. She instinctively put a hand up to her face. Instead of feeling gratified at his observation as she had done at the exhibition, she now felt extremely plain and unalluring. Maybe she should spend the evening in her room and leave him free to dine with someone more attractive.

'So, here's your key. We'll meet in an hour. That suit you?'

Sandy hesitated again.

'If you'd rather be doing something else, rather than spending the evening with me, I mean — '

She felt the colour return to her face in a rush as her words petered out lamely. This was mainly due to Oliver's quizzically amused expression.

'Why would I want to be doing something else?'

He tilted his head to one side as he studied her, paying special attention, she felt, to the high colour of her cheeks.

'Well, I've heard that Birmingham is

a wonderful city to spend the evening in. You know, night clubs and such.'

'Sandy,' he said and smiled slowly at her, 'there's nothing I'd hate more, unless, of course, you'd rather be doing that.'

'Oh, no, no, definitely not. A quiet evening in will suit me.'

'Good, because I can't think of a better way to spend the time.'

Heavy lids hooded his expression now but not before she'd glimpsed the warmth of his look.

'So, see you in an hour, in the bar.'

7

Sandy lay in the bath, turning the last few moments' conversation over in her mind. She had to be wrong. He was just being kind. Yet, as much as she was modifying her low opinion of him, it still seemed extremely unlikely. No, a much more plausible explanation was that he was as tired as she was but he just was more adept at concealing it.

Eventually, she climbed out of the bath. She'd come prepared this time. Her little black dress was already laid out on the bed. It wasn't new, or particularly fashionable, but it was the only garment she possessed that could be remotely classified as informal evening wear.

Regarding it now, with her head to one side, she just hoped it wasn't too dressy. This hotel wasn't what she had hoped for when she'd booked it. In fact, it looked the sort of place where people would come down for dinner in jeans and sweaters. Oh, well, she sighed, too late now. She hadn't brought anything else with her. The dress would have to do.

She slipped it over her head and then applied her make-up and did her hair. The final touch was her favourite perfume. Again, she eyed herself in the mirror. She suspected that Oliver Carlton possessed a very critical eye where women were concerned, especially women who were dining out with him. Would she live up to his rigorous standards? Oh, well, if she didn't it was just too bad.

She shrugged as she turned away from her reflection. This evening was only concerned with business when all was said and done. For all her nonchalance, though, she couldn't help but feel nervous, because business or not, she was still about to spend the evening in a handsome man's company — a man, moreover, she was in deep danger of loving if her feelings when she was with him lately were anything to go by. Still, she wouldn't be natural if she didn't feel some anticipation at the prospect.

Oliver was already in the bar. He'd got himself a newspaper from somewhere, the Financial Times, she saw, and was reading while he sipped a gin and tonic. He didn't see her right away so it gave Sandy the opportunity to study him without him being aware of it.

He was good-looking, even more so than usual. Dressed in a tan shirt, with a shade darker jacket and trousers, he exuded sex appeal. The colours emphasised his colouring. Oliver Carlton was certainly a man to be reckoned with and one she was suddenly proud to be spending the evening with.

That sentiment could have had something to do with the way that two women sitting at another table were appraising him. They were talking excitedly, laughing loudly, their gestures animated and exaggerated. Clearly they were trying very hard to attract Oliver's attention. Oliver, however, seemed oblivious to the interest he was arousing.

Sandy felt her heartbeat quicken and she walked across to him.

'Oliver?'

She sensed rather than saw the women's disappointment and she couldn't suppress the thrill of triumph. As she had feared, they were dressed casually, but in that moment of euphoria, it didn't seem to matter.

Oliver looked up as she approached him. He instantly got to his feet, folding the newspaper as he did so.

'Let me get you that drink. Vodka tonic, wasn't it?'

Sandy experienced a helpless stab of pleasure at the fact that he'd remembered. Stop it, she told herself. She wasn't here on a date with him. She was his PA, for goodness' sake, and he was simply being polite. It was a sobering thought and one that dashed her spirits, as was the subsequent notion that she shouldn't be harbouring such sentiments about the man who had all but destroyed her father. Whatever was she thinking of?

Oliver placed the drink before her, saying, 'You look better, less tired.'

She didn't know whether she should take that as a compliment or not. It would depend on how she'd looked before her bath, she supposed. Nonetheless, and despite the turmoil of her emotions, she managed a fleeting smile before taking a mouthful of her drink.

'Are you hungry?' he asked.

'Starving.'

'Come on then. Let's take our drinks through to the dining-room. The menu looks quite good. I snatched a look on the way to the bar.'

They were shown to a table in the corner of the room, a dark corner but for the large, white candle burning in the centre of the table. It gave a very intimate look to things, too intimate, in Sandy's opinion. They were only employer and employee, when all was said and done.

Oliver, however, didn't look at all

bothered. He was probably perfectly accustomed to dining by candlelight with a woman. It was only Sandy who was getting flustered, once again revealing her lack of sophistication, she supposed. It wasn't that she'd never before dined with a man by candlelight, she had. The fact was she'd never before dined with her boss in such a romantic situation and it was completely unnerving her.

Once they were seated and their order taken by the waiter, Sandy sipped gingerly at her drink. Other people were starting to drift in and take their places at the tables and she was relieved to see that several of the women were dressed elegantly so she didn't feel quite as out of place as she had expected. More candles were being lit, which meant that the room took on a little more brightness.

'Who are we going to see tomorrow?' she asked, striving to relieve the sense of intimacy that still prevailed, despite the better light.

'Let's not talk business,' Oliver remarked, leaning back in his seat and subjecting her to close scrutiny. 'I've had my fill of that for today. I make it a practice to relax in the evening. I like to recharge the old batteries.'

Sandy felt rebuffed, reprimanded, almost.

'S — sorry,' she stammered.

'Don't be,' Oliver told her smoothly.

He lifted his glass to his mouth, continuing to study her over its rim as he did so.

The candlelight was casting shadows, making his features look more defined, harsher, yet, at the same time, intensifying the glitter in his eye. He looked more like the man that his reputation had suggested.

'Tell me, Sandy, what happened to your father?'

Sandy stiffened. That was the last question that she'd expected. It was more of a bombshell, actually. She gave heartfelt thanks for the lack of light. Hopefully, it would hide her sense of shock.

'My father?' she stammered.

'Yes. Portia seemed to think he was in Spain. In fact, she implied he'd run away.'

'Oh, I see.'

Sandy's thoughts swirled. What on earth was she going to say now, without giving away Oliver's own part in events? Maybe she should be honest with him, see what he had to say for himself. No, such barefaced criticism would surely lead to the loss of her own job and she couldn't afford that, not with a family to take care of.

'Um, no, he hasn't run away. I don't know where Portia got that idea from. He went to work in a bar in Spain, she did get that bit right.'

She attempted a cool smile, but it didn't work. She felt her lips twist into a sort of grimace instead.

'He began it with a friend, who promised him a partnership but it didn't work out.'

'But why haven't you all gone? Where is he now?'

'He's moving around a bit so — '

At that point, the waiter arrived with their first course. Sandy could have thrown her arms around him, so great was her relief at this timely interruption. By the time the plates were set down and the bottle of wine Oliver had ordered was duly opened and poured, she felt she could change the subject without appearing to be obviously dodging the issue.

'Tell me about your family,' she invited.

Oliver, of course, knew what she was doing. His measured glance told her that. However, he must have decided to respect her reluctance to talk about her father.

'Well, my parents have retired to Portugal. They bought a villa, close to a golf course. My father spends the larger part of his day on that, my mother spends her time playing bridge.'

'How lovely,' she said.

She still felt uncomfortable. Oliver was being so open about his family, while she, well, she had her secrets.

'Do you have any brothers or sisters?' she asked brightly.

'One sister.'

He was smiling, making no pretence of anything other than amusement at her patently artificial manner. 'She's married, with two children. She lives in Edinburgh, having married a Scotsman. That's what I miss,' he mused suddenly.

'What? Living in Scotland?'

'No.'

He chuckled, a deep, throaty sound and caused a spasm of excitement to curl round Sandy's stomach.

'Having some children. That's the price one pays for staying single.'

'But you've been married,' she blurted out.

Whatever had possessed her to say a thing like that? She felt the blood drain from her face as she waited for his response. When it came, however, it was nothing like the rebuke she had expected. He simply smiled, ruefully.

'Yes, once, long ago,' he said. 'At

least, that's how it feels.'

'I'm sorry. I shouldn't have — it's absolutely none of my business.'

'It's all right. I'm not ashamed of it.'

Was he implying that she was ashamed of her family because she refused to talk about her father? But that was different. That, if he only knew it, was all down to him. How on earth could she say that to him?

'I was twenty-three, she was barely nineteen. Far too young, of course.'

Sandy noted his failure to specify which one of them it was who had been too young, himself or his bride. Maybe he meant both of them, although she was quite sure that Oliver, even at twenty-three, would have known precisely what and whom he wanted.

'It lasted all of eighteen months before we decided to call it quits, a mutual decision. We were totally incompatible. We wanted different things. I wanted children, eventually, she didn't.'

His words tailed off as a brooding, melancholy look came over him. He lowered his gaze away from hers for the first time, and he looked as if he were studying the pattern on the tablecloth. All the while, his long fingers toyed with the stem of his wine glass.

'I'm sorry,' she said.

'Oh, don't be. I'm not, not now, at least. It would never have lasted.'

He looked back at her.

'Do you plan on getting married? Or has this Jon put you off?'

'Oh, no. I've just never met anyone I wanted to marry.'

Till now — the words echoed so loudly inside her head, she couldn't be sure she hadn't spoken them out loud.

'I see. So you will, sometime then?'

He looked unusually keen to hear her reply. Sandy was puzzled. Why should it matter to him whether she married or not?

'I expect so, some day.'

Then, she, too, lapsed into silence.

'More wine?' he asked, lifting up the bottle.

To Sandy's astonishment, she saw

that her glass was empty. When had she drunk all of that?

'Yes, please.'

She'd drink this more slowly. In fact, she'd make it last throughout the meal. She didn't want to do what she'd done the last time they'd dined together, when she'd certainly had more than she was used to. It had blurred her judgement, loosened her tongue, and she didn't want that happening this evening, not if Oliver was going to be asking more sensitive questions about her family. Who knew what she might end up telling him?

He didn't ask any more questions, however, and once the meal was over, Sandy decided to get out while the going was good and retire to her room.

When she said as much, Oliver said, 'Good idea. I think I'll do the same.'

When he gave a quizzical smile, Sandy found herself recalling the previous occasion when they'd stayed in a hotel together and he'd made the mistake of telling her he'd join her. It was evident he was remembering the same thing. Sandy felt herself blushing.

'I can't recall the last time I saw a woman blush,' Oliver murmured.

They were walking towards the lift that would take them to the second floor and their rooms. By the time they reached it, Sandy's face was flaming. She raced inside the lift, quite unable to speak.

'I've embarrassed you even further now, haven't I? I don't know why. It's a charming thing to do. I wish more women did it.'

Sandy kept her eyes downcast. The space inside the lift was too small for comfort. She felt confined, hemmed in, mainly because they were forced to stand, shoulder touching shoulder. She was so close to him she could feel the heat of his body, smell his aftershave.

It seemed even more intense than usual in this limited space. Her head spun. Oh, no! She must have drunk more wine than she'd thought, after all. She put out a hand to press the floor button at the same moment that Oliver did, wanting nothing more than to be alone, in her room, and safe.

Their fingers touched. Oliver turned his hand quickly, clasping hers in his. He then lifted his other hand and pressed the button. The doors closed as he turned slowly to face her.

'Sandy.'

The voice was low, throaty. His eyes blazed into hers, compelling, golden, almost. He was still holding her hand. His fingers caressed the back of it. Sandy's breathing went wild, catapulting her pulse into hyperdrive. Frantic to try and calm her madly spiralling emotions, she wriggled her fingers in his, trying to free herself. She gave a little gasp, for Oliver was tightening his grip. He began to pull her closer. Sandy resisted, in vain.

'I've wanted to do this for so long now,' he murmured huskily.

'What?'

Sandy's voice sounded strangled. She began to tremble. She was staring into eyes that were like deep pools, impenetrable, giving nothing of his intentions away.

'This,' he said.

Without another word, he slid an arm about her waist, and lowered his head to hers.

Sandy literally froze, quite unable to move. In the next second, Oliver's mouth was pressing upon hers, gently at first, then, searchingly, demandingly, forcing a response from her.

Sandy's eyes stayed open to start with, as she stared helplessly into Oliver's tawny depths. Then, as she watched, spellbound by what was happening, his lids lowered, concealing his expression from her as his grip upon her tightened. Sandy couldn't help herself. She sighed softly, almost imperceptibly, and wound her arms around his neck, clinging on to him for dear life, returning his kiss with everything that was inside her.

All her deepest emotions sprang into being, the emotions that she had been struggling so hard to suppress. She was helpless against their heightened intensity, against him.

His hold on her tightened yet again as he pinned her to him. Sandy's breathing quickened, then slowed, as their kiss deepened. She was powerless to halt things. A warmth, the like of which she'd never felt before, began deep in her stomach. A bell tinged somewhere and she was dimly aware of doors sliding open.

It took a woman's soft voice, murmuring, 'Oh, my!' to awaken her to the realisation of where she was and what she was doing! It was then, and only then, that Sandy opened her eyes, to flick her gaze to the right, only to see an elderly couple standing outside the lift, beaming delightedly at her and Oliver. She gasped and jerked her head backwards, so vigorously that her head spun once more. The kiss, not unexpectedly, ended as abruptly as it had begun.

Oliver, visibly startled, exclaimed, 'Sandy!' before he, too, glanced to one side and, in a flash of understanding, said, 'Oh!'

'Don't mind us,' the elderly gentleman

assured them. 'It's nice to see two people so happy.'

That did it. Sandy didn't wait to hear any more. Mortified almost beyond endurance, she fled from the lift and along the corridor to the door of her room. She did hear Oliver saying something indistinguishable to the couple, after which they chuckled. Oh, no! He was joking about it! How could he? It was obviously all just a game to him.

With shaking fingers, she eventually managed to unlock her door and swiftly stepped inside, just in time. She'd barely closed it behind her to stand, hands over her face, wondering how on earth she was going to face him again after this, when Oliver's voice reached her. He must be standing right outside her door.

'Sandy? Please open the door.'

Sandy didn't answer. She couldn't. There was nothing to say, in any case. How could she possibly explain her response to him, her complete surrender? It was impossible. She couldn't even explain it to herself. If Lucy or her mother ever found out!

'Sandy, open this door.'

It was the voice of the employer, rather than the lover, inflexible, refusing to take no for an answer. It gave Sandy the strength to reply.

'Please, go away, Oliver.'

'Not until you open this door. I'm sorry.'

'Don't be.'

She couldn't believe her voice when she spoke. It was light, unconcerned. Where had that come from?

'It was just a kiss, that was all. Probably the result of a little too much wine.'

'Sandy, for goodness' sake!'

'Good-night, Oliver.'

With that, she moved into the room, to pull her suitcase out from the bottom of the wardrobe where she'd temporarily stored it. She knew, without doubt, what she had to do now. There was no way she would be able to carry on tomorrow as if nothing had happened between them. She'd get the train back to Wilmsley first thing in the morning. He'd have to manage tomorrow without her. She'd leave a note at reception for him.

It would probably earn her the sack this time. After all, this was twice now she'd run out on him, a sin of truly unforgiveable proportions in Oliver's book, she was sure. But she couldn't help it. She had to go. She desperately needed a breathing space, mainly to come to terms with what that kiss had revealed.

She gave a small sob. She couldn't believe what she'd allowed to happen. She'd only gone and fallen in love, head over heels in love, actually with Oliver Carlton!

8

Sandy got off the train the following morning and decided that, instead of getting a taxi, she'd walk to work. It wasn't far, a half a mile or so, and the chilly morning air would clear her head, hopefully, go some way towards wiping out all memories of Oliver's devastating kiss the evening before.

She'd be a bit earlier than usual. It was only half past eight now, but she'd been up at the crack of dawn, determined to be gone from the hotel before her employer arrived down for breakfast. She just hoped that he'd got her note and hadn't been too furious with her.

The main thing was this way, she'd be able to catch up on the work she'd missed doing yesterday. She wanted everything in order and completely up to date in the likely event that Oliver dismissed her.

She couldn't see what alternative he had, not really. She'd walked out on him, an act that would, in his book, be tantamount to treason, she was sure. It really wasn't like her. She might be many things, but a coward had never been one of them, not until now, that is, but the truth was she just hadn't felt able to face him, not this morning, not with the memory of the passion they'd shared so overwhelmingly still so vivid.

She had to walk through the town to get to Meredith's, right past the Odd Spot Café, where the smell of freshly-brewed coffee drew her towards its door. She'd go in and have some breakfast. Work could wait another fifteen minutes or so. She turned to open the door and that was when she saw them — Lucy and Jon, sitting just back from the window, their heads close together, talking animatedly.

She pushed open the door and strode across to them. She wondered if Felicity knew Lucy was here. Had she given her permission? Sandy had tried to tell her mother how unhappy she was about her sister consorting with a man so much older than herself but Felicity hadn't seemed unduly bothered.

'Oh, darling,' she'd sighed, 'it's just a crush. She'll soon get over it. Anyway, I'm not so sure that I wouldn't rather she was with Jon than that other individual you caught her with.'

Sandy had sighed with frustration. This wasn't the first time that Felicity had shown a lamentable lack of judgement over Lucy's wayward behaviour. It was the main reason why Sandy, to her sister's disgust, tried to instruct and guide Lucy.

Felicity could be foolishly indulgent where her youngest daughter was concerned.

It had maddened Sandy more than once, as well as caused her quite a few pangs of hurt over the years. Felicity had been much stricter with her. Now, she found herself asking whether they were actively conspiring against her?

Neither Lucy nor Jon saw her at first. In fact, she'd reached the table and was standing over them before Lucy glanced up.

'What are you doing here?' she asked crossly.

'More to the point, what are you doing here?' was Sandy's response to that. 'Shouldn't you be at college?'

'No. I have a free period. Anyway, why shouldn't I be here?'

Lucy frowned up at her sister.

'I thought you weren't back till this evening. Are you spying on me?'

'Of course not,' Sandy replied indignantly. 'I decided to return early. Lots to do.'

'Huh! And what did the high-and-mighty Oliver Carlton have to say about that? He can't seem to blow his nose without you there to wipe it for him.'

Up to this point, Jon hadn't uttered a single word. Sandy now swung her head to stare at him.

'And shouldn't you be at work? Or have they sacked you, already?'

He gave a low chuckle.

'Yeah, you'd like that, wouldn't you?'

Sandy shrugged.

'Don't flatter yourself. I couldn't care less.'

Jon gave a disbelieving smile.

'I've got an early appointment, with one of our customers so they're not expecting me in yet.'

'Oh, I see.'

'Disappointed, sister?' Lucy asked sarcastically. 'I know you hate us meeting.'

Sandy met her defiant gaze.

'Don't you think he's a little old for you, Lucy?'

'What is it with you? I was with Damian and that was wrong. Now, I'm with someone more sensible and that's wrong, too. What do you want, Sandy?'

Sandy opened her mouth to reply but Lucy cut her off.

'I know you warned him off.'

Jon put out a hand to try and calm her.

'Lucy . . . '

'Oh, save it. I'm going anyway. I'll see you later, Jon.'

She got to her feet, at the same time glaring defiantly at her older sister.

'Lucy, please, listen.'

'No. You know what your trouble is, don't you, Sandy? You're just jealous. You blew it. Now it's my turn and you can't stand that, can you?'

'No, that's not how it is. I'm worried about you.'

She darted a sideways glance at Jon. He was grinning once more, smugly.

'Oh, yeah, sure you are. The only thing you're worried about is that I might be getting what you now can't have. Well, tough.'

She bent down towards Jon.

'See you later, honey,' and with that she placed a deliberately sensual kiss upon Jon's still grinning mouth.

Once Lucy had gone, Jon waved Sandy to the vacant seat.

'Sit down. I think you and I should have a little talk.'

'How right you are.'

Sandy sat down and, with both elbows on the table top, leaned towards the man sitting opposite.

'Jon, I'm begging you, leave Lucy alone. She's too young, too vulnerable, and too inexperienced.'

Jon threw back his head and laughed.

'Too inexperienced! That's a joke. She's unlike her sister who couldn't bear me to touch her.'

Sandy gasped.

'If you lay one finger on her — '

'There's one way you can end things between her and me.'

Sandy stared at him.

'How?'

'You come back to me, Sandy. That way, I'll have no need of Lucy. It's very simple. Prove how much you care for her.'

Sandy snatched her hand away from his.

'I'd sooner die.'

'Well, in that case, things stay as they are. I agree Lucy's too young for me. I like 'em a bit more mature but in the absence of that — '

Sandy leaped to her feet, rocking the table, making the cups rattle in their saucers.

'That's blackmail.'

Jon again laughed at her.

'Yeah, so it is. But it's the only way I'll leave Lucy alone, so think about it.'

'I don't need to think about it, Jon. As I said a few moments ago, I'd rather die. No, it's Lucy I'll talk to. She'll see sense. I'll make sure of that.'

'I wouldn't bet on it. In her eyes I can do no wrong so she certainly won't believe any tales you might decide to tell her.'

In the end, and despite all of her good intentions, Sandy was actually late arriving at Meredith's. After leaving Jon, she'd felt unable to face going straight to work, her head whirling, her thoughts in chaos. What was she going to do? She couldn't go back to Jon, not even for Lucy's sake.

She was sitting at her desk later that morning, catching up on the work as she'd set out to do, when to her astonishment, Oliver walked in. He strode straight past her, ignoring her gasp of surprise, not even breaking his stride as he spoke.

'My office, now, please, Sandy.'

Sandy noticed that he didn't as much as glance her way, which, to her, in her acutely sensitive state indicated immediate dismissal. He must have left the hotel the instant he received her note to have got back by this time, which meant he hadn't been to see the people he'd intended visiting, even more reason to dismiss her.

With a quaking heart and legs that trembled, Sandy followed him, taking care to close the door between their offices. June had a habit of just walking into her room, without as much as a knock, and Sandy didn't want anyone to overhear what she suspected was about to happen.

'Sit down.'

Oliver pointed her to the chair that faced him across his desk top. Sandy decided to take the bull by the horns and get in first. If she resigned, it would look a whole lot better on her CV than dismissal would, and she did have her future to think of.

'Oliver, I — ' she began, somewhat tentatively.

She hadn't meant to sound like that. She'd intended being firm, self-confident. But Oliver didn't appear to hear her because he pre-empted anything she might have to stay with words of his own, equally tentatively, to Sandy's surprise.

'I want to apologise, Sandy. The fault was all mine. I'm sorry. Last night makes it twice now that I seem to have succeeded in driving you away. I realise I placed you in an impossible position. I'm so sorry. I couldn't seem to help myself. Nonetheless, that's no excuse. You had just cause to desert me. We have to work together and I must have embarrassed you, terribly, especially, as we were caught in the act, so to speak.'

Hot colour rushed to Sandy's face. What was it about this man, that he had the power to make her blush so hotly, so frequently, something she hadn't done since she was a teenager. Embarrassed all over again, she burst into words.

'No, really, it's OK. It wasn't that bad.'

She could have bitten her tongue out. It only took her a second to recognise the interpretation he was likely to place upon that guileless remark. His low mutter confirmed her suspicion.

'Well, thanks. I must be losing my touch.'

In an effort to right the wrong she'd done him, because, of all the men she'd kissed in her life, Oliver Carlton had been the most expert, the most exciting, the most arousing that she'd ever experienced. However, she could hardly say that to him.

'Look, let's just forget it. I already have,' she rushed on.

She chewed frantically at her bottom lip. He didn't look any too pleased by that either. She was saying all the wrong things! She couldn't seem to stop herself. It must be the sheer relief that he wasn't sacking her, although, at the rate she was going, she wasn't out of the woods yet.

Oliver looked almost hurt, in some inexplicable way. His next words intensified that impression.

'Right, I see. Forget it.'

He turned his head away from her, but she would have sworn he said, in a low voice, so she might not have heard correctly, 'That might be easier said than done.'

Again, Sandy was puzzled. Surely, he'd be as eager as she was to forget everything that had happened between them. When he could have a woman as glamorous as Portia in his arms, why on earth would he want her, ordinary little Sandy Owen?

However, she didn't have time to work that one out, as intriguing as the question might be, for Oliver was handing her a stack of papers and business cards. It was the stuff from the exhibition that they needed to follow up on.

'Perhaps you'd deal with these.'

His glance now was a steely one, cold, one might almost say, and his jawline, always firm, had now assumed the properties of a granite block.

Sandy's heart ached as she pondered the fact that she had in some way wounded him with her nonchalant attitude to their kiss. But that had to be ridiculous, didn't it? He couldn't possibly feel the same way that she did.

As if she hadn't got enough problems of her own to contend with, it was soon after that that Meredith's began to lose orders, several very substantial orders, the last nine to be precise.

Sandy had submitted her quotes as normal and then heard nothing. One or two she expected to lose, maybe even half of them. It was, after all, par for the course, but to lose all of them was highly unusual. Coincidentally, they'd all been sent at the same time. At first, she wondered if they could have been lost in the post. It seemed unlikely but it was worth checking on.

Taking matters into her own hands, she rang each one of the firms involved. Since the debacle of the exhibition, and their talk afterwards, Oliver had grown far too remote for her to bother him with something like this. In fact, she'd barely seen him since. She didn't know whether that was a relief or not. All she did know was that she missed him.

The prospective customers, to a man, told her that in every case Carrington's had got the order. They'd consistently underquoted Meredith's prices so naturally, they'd given the order to them. All of this led Sandy to suspect industrial espionage, from which point it didn't take her long to work out who must be responsible.

It had to be Jon! It was too much of a coincidence not to be. He'd started working for Carrington's and Meredith's was now being underquoted on practically ever order. It had never, ever happened before, not in all the time that Sandy had been at Meredith's. Somehow, he must have known, in advance, what Meredith's prices would be. But how could he have known that?

She thought back. She'd taken every one of those files with the drawings and estimates home with her to look over and re-check their totals. It wasn't something she normally did but there seemed so much work to do lately that she simply hadn't had the time during the day. Home was much quieter, with no interruptions, but even so, how would Jon have known?

An awful thought occurred to her. It wouldn't have been impossible for Lucy to sneak a look at them. Sandy hadn't locked them away, not deeming it necessary in her own home. Lucy was still seeing Jon, she knew. The younger girl hadn't made any attempt to hide the fact. If anything, she had gloated about it.

Nonetheless, Sandy had decided to say nothing more to Lucy, to simply wait and hope that the affair burned out of its own accord. Lucy was notorious, after all, for losing interest fairly rapidly in things and people. But now, in the light of what she suspected was happening, she wondered if she'd been wise.

Lucy could so easily have made a note of the facts and figures and passed them on to Jon. She didn't want to think that but she couldn't see how it had happened any other way. Apart from Sandy, only June had seen the quotes when she typed them up ready for mailing, and she would trust June over anyone, even her own sister.

That evening, she confronted Lucy. To her horror, Lucy admitted freely what she'd done.

'Why, Lucy? Why?'

'To revenge myself, on Oliver Carlton, on behalf of Dad. If I can be instrumental in any way in his downfall — '

'You stupid girl! This is my job you're jeopardising. Did Jon put you up to this?'

Lucy looked away.

'He did, didn't he?'

'No, it was my idea. He just agreed to help me.'

'And, of course, it was nothing to do with helping himself at the same time — to what? Possible promotion? More money?'

'Well, so what? If it gives us a better life together.'

'What? Oh, Lucy, can't you see Jon for what he is? He's an opportunist. He'll drop you like a hot brick as soon as he's had his fill of you.'

'You know your trouble, don't you?' Lucy shouted. 'I've said it before and I'll say it again. You're jealous because it's me he wants now, not you.'

'That's not true,' Sandy insisted. 'Jon and I were finished a long time ago.'

'Yeah, he said. He couldn't stand your coldness any longer.'

'Is that what he told you? That he finished it?'

'Yes.'

Sandy stayed silent for a moment, and then made a decision. She couldn't stand by and see her young sister involved with someone who would do what Jon was doing. She didn't believe it was all Lucy's idea. If Jon could bankrupt Meredith's, it would be a perfect revenge for Jon as well as Lucy. Sandy would be out of a job and it would be solely down to him.

'Lucy, it wasn't Jon who finished things, it was me and the reason was I found out that he'd been having affairs with other women all the time I was seeing him. When I confronted him with what I'd discovered he became extremely abusive. I don't want to see you hurt.'

'You're lying,' Lucy screamed. 'Jon wouldn't do that. He'd never hurt me, never. He'd never hurt anyone. I don't believe it. Is there nothing you wouldn't do, or say, to spoil things for me? Well, you won't put me off him and if there's anything else I can do to help him and harm Oliver Carlton, then I'll do it.'

'What if I tell Oliver what you've done?' Of course, she never would, but Lucy didn't know that. It seemed to work.

For the first time, Lucy looked afraid.

'You wouldn't. You'd take his side against me, your own sister? I did it for us, for you, me, Mum.'

'No, you did it for you, Lucy, nobody else.'

Sandy lay awake for a long time that night, turning everything over and over in her head. If she told Oliver what had happened and that it was Jon responsible for the loss of all the orders, he'd probably go to the police, and that would surely mean the fraud squad. They'd arrest Jon, who, if she knew Jon, would then implicate Lucy. She couldn't do it, not to her own sister.

She'd have to resign. It was the only honourable thing to do. It was her fault it had all happened because she'd taken the work home and then carelessly left it lying around. How could she go on working at Meredith's and, maybe, at some time in the future, risk the same thing happening again? She couldn't. She'd have to take responsibility, as she couldn't reveal that Jon was the culprit, and leave.

So, with her mind made up, she went downstairs the next morning, only to be greeted by her mother.

'Sandy, darling, I'm going to Spain for a little holiday. You'll be OK here, won't you? You can keep an eye on Lucy.'

'Sure. When are you going?'

'This afternoon.'

'This afternoon! For goodness' sake, why didn't you say anything till now?'

Felicity looked evasive, uncomfortable.

'I didn't want to say anything in case it all fell through, and you've looked so preoccupied, I didn't want to bother you with my plans. I've managed to pick up a last-minute cancellation.'

'Last minute is right. Who are you going with? Joan?'

'No.'

Her mother again looked uncomfortable. For the first time then, Sandy wondered if there could be a man involved in this somewhere. Yes, that must be it, and her mother was too embarrassed to admit to it. Joan had been giving her an alibi which was why Joan had also looked shifty and ill-at-ease the day Sandy spoke to her. It all made sense.

Sandy smiled at her mother, instantly forgiving her for her secrecy. It was time Felicity had some fun again and it didn't look as if her father was going to come back, although, in the event of her resigning from Meredith's it would have been nice to have her mother to talk to, to share her problems with. Oh, well, she mustn't be selfish and spoil her mother's pleasure. Time enough for her to know about Sandy's troubles when she got home again.

9

A grim-faced and steely-eyed Oliver was waiting for Sandy when she arrived at work. With a sinking heart, she wondered if he could have heard about the loss of orders.

He had!

'I'd like to know what you think of our losing nine orders in total, near enough sixty thousand pounds worth of business, to Carrington's. I'd also like you to tell me how you think it happened. Apparently, in each case, we were narrowly undercut in price, which leads me to suspect they had some sort of inside information about our costings. How do you account for that?'

'I can't, I'm afraid.'

Sandy began to tremble. She couldn't incriminate Jon, and therefore her sister, she simply couldn't.

'In which case, I'm tendering my

resignation,' she added.

At a stroke, the colour drained from Oliver's face. Even his lips turned white.

'Are you admitting it was you?'

He spoke so quietly it was all she could do to hear the words.

'No, but it was my responsibility. I'm the one who did the quotations. They were in my possession right up until I posted them, apart from when June typed them, of course.'

He opened his mouth to speak but Sandy cut him off.

'And I would trust June with my life.'

That seemed to floor him. He didn't speak for several moments.

'Sandy, there's really no need for you to resign, if you can assure me you weren't to blame.'

'I can't, though, you see.'

'Did you take the paperwork out of the factory at any time?'

Sandy hesitated.

'Only to my home, nowhere else, and I brought them back here the next day.'

'I see. Is there any possibility . . . '

She could see which way his mind was working. It wouldn't take him long to get to Lucy and from there to Jon.

Hastily, she said, 'It's totally down to me, Oliver, totally. So, I'll leave at the end of the week, if that's OK, or right now, if you'd rather.'

Her voice broke at that and tears stung her eyes. Hastily, she dashed them away. She knew what he was thinking. There was no other conclusion he could come to. She'd told him it was totally down to her, a tacit admission of guilt in his eyes, she was sure. All she could do now was hope he didn't call the police.

Oliver had turned away so he didn't see this display of emotion.

'You do what you want, Sandy.'

His voice was dispassionate, clinically so. It was as if he could no longer bear to look at her, much less speak to her, and no wonder. She'd more or less admitted to being a thief.

'In that case, it might be best if I

went immediately.'

A small sob quivered in her throat as the greatest sense of loss she'd ever experienced hit her. Her heart lurched with sickening ferocity. She'd probably never see him again. She'd have no reason to and their paths were unlikely to cross. They didn't exactly mix in the same social circles.

She didn't waste any time. Didn't they say clean breaks were the best? Swiftly and unobtrusively, she cleared her desk. Even June didn't realise she was leaving for good. Moments later, with a single, despairing glance round, she took her final leave.

From then on, the days passed slowly, agonisingly so. Sandy was appalled at the pain she felt at the notion that Oliver believed she was the one responsible for the leaks. Surely, he would have known she wasn't capable of something like that. But she'd as good as told him she was. What else was he to think?

She tried desperately to find another job but there was nothing available of the same calibre and wage as her position at Meredith's and without a reference from the only firm she'd ever worked for, as she hadn't been able to bring herself to ask Oliver for one, it was unlikely that she'd be successful, even if she discovered a vacancy that was suitable. She didn't know what she was going to do. How would they manage without her wage? It didn't bear thinking about.

She hadn't heard from her mother, not as much as a postcard, although Felicity knew what had happened. She'd still been at home when Sandy had returned from Meredith's so Sandy had had no option but to tell her she was out of work. She hadn't seemed worried, however. Her thoughts were completely taken up with her forthcoming trip.

'He didn't sack you, did he?' she asked.

'No, I resigned.'

'Oh, well, I'm sure you'll soon find something else, darling. And really, when all's said and done, I'd really rather you weren't working for that man.'

It had been Lucy who'd shown the most emotion.

'You resigned? Why?' she asked in amazement.

'Why do you think?' Sandy had replied bitterly. 'It was down to my carelessness that you obtained the information to give to Jon, so that makes it my responsibility.'

'But there was no need for you to resign. You could have simply pleaded ignorance about the whole thing. Did he blame you?'

For the first time, Lucy showed signs of uncertainty, shame, even.

'Not in so many words.'

'Oh, Sandy, I never thought, not for a minute — '

'No, you never do, Lucy,' Sandy quietly put in. 'That's the problem.'

The day that Felicity was due back from Spain, Sandy got up early, determined to have the house looking like a new pin to welcome her mother home. After all, she gave a hollow laugh, she had nothing else to do.

She'd almost finished the last bedroom when she heard the sound of a taxi cab and her mother's laughing tones. A man's voice replied. She laughed softly to herself. She'd been right then, a man was involved. She felt happy for her mother, at least. She tripped down the stairs and flung open the front door, preparing herself to greet a possibly prospective partner for her mother.

'Why, Sandy, darling, there you are. No job yet then?'

But Sandy wasn't listening. Her eyes were glued to the man standing just to one side of Felicity, bent over, paying the cab driver. Even from his back view, Sandy had no problem recognising him. It was Martin Owen, her father!

It wasn't until the four of them, Martin, Felicity, Sandy and Lucy were sitting over dinner that evening that Felicity said, 'Girls, your father has something to tell you both, especially you, Sandy.'

Sandy was startled.

'Me?'

'Yes,' Martin began. 'A confession. I should have done it in the beginning but, well, I didn't.'

Nervously, he cleared his throat. He couldn't seem to look at Sandy. Sandy felt her heart lurch. What was coming now? She didn't think she could take much more.

'I wasn't made redundant when Carlton bought us out. His accountant discovered several discrepancies in the accounts, not to put too fine a point on it.'

He looked shame-facedly at them all.

'I'd been fiddling the books. That's how I could afford the big house, the car, everything. They threatened to call the police in the first instance but I pleaded that I had a family, and all else. Anyway, the long and short of it was Carlton himself came to see me and agreed to take no further action if I left immediately and started to pay back the money, which I did to begin with. They were pretty good, really. They even paid me redundancy which they didn't have to do in the circumstances. I think that was down to Carlton again. He was concerned about my family.

'I don't think he's as bad as he's been painted, you know. Anyway, when Sam offered me the job in Spain, it seemed like a chance to start afresh. That was a joke. Some fresh start! All he wanted was a barman, not a partner. The bar never made enough money so he was forced to cut my wages, which meant I couldn't afford to carry on paying off my debt to Carlton. Then, when Sam told me he couldn't make me a partner either, not without a large infusion of cash, which I hadn't got, I lost it, I'm afraid. We had an almighty row and, well, you know the rest. I walked out.'

'Oh, Dad. Why didn't you just come home?' Sandy exclaimed.

'I couldn't face you all with yet another failure under my belt. I decided you'd all be better off without me so I ran away.'

Sandy blindly reached for her father's hand and squeezed it. In a way, she could understand how he'd felt. Hadn't she run away, too, from the strength of her feelings, as well as from Oliver?

'How did Mum find you?'

Martin smiled and nodded at his wife and Felicity took up the tale.

'Joan and her husband had been holidaying in Spain, and they recognised Martin working in another bar. She told me, gave me the name of the bar and the phone number and I rang them. Your father answered and, hey presto! That's why I've been going to Joan's, not to go out but to receive your father's phone calls. He'd ring here briefly to let me know he had some time to talk and I would rush around to Joan's to phone him back.'

'But why the secrecy? I don't understand.'

'It was your father's wish. He didn't want to build your hopes up if we couldn't work things out between us. He'd told me the real reason why he was sacked. He believed you'd be so ashamed of him. That's why I went to see him, face to face, to convince him that he was wrong, that we'd all missed him, that you'd both be overjoyed to see him again.'

'Was your mother right?' Martin asked nervously.

Words didn't seem enough. Both of his daughters rushed to him and put their arms about him.

*   *   *

If things had got better for her mother and sister, they hadn't as far as Sandy was concerned. She spent several more fruitless days trying to find work. She'd more or less made up her mind to take anything, just to bring in some money. Her father hadn't decided what he was going to do yet, although he had a couple of ideas for a business of his own, if he could just persuade the bank to trust him and lend him some start-up money. Whatever he decided to do, his family would be behind him. They'd all made that clear.

None of this, of course, helped Sandy. She was in the depths of despair. So when a couple of afternoons later, she arrived home, even more dispirited than usual, to find an anxious Felicity waiting for her on the front doorstep, all she could think was, what now?

'Sandy,' her mother whispered, 'just to warn you. Oliver Carlton's here. Lucy's with him. They've been talking for an hour or more. I don't know what about. She wouldn't tell me.'

Sandy was conscious of a sinking feeling in the pit of her stomach. Oh, no! What had Lucy done now?

'OK. I'll go in and see what's going on.'

She walked quickly to the door that led into the sitting-room and threw it open. Oliver was sitting in one armchair, Lucy in the other. Lucy's expression confirmed every one of Sandy's worst fears.

'I went to Meredith's this morning, Sandy. Your assistant, June, rang Oliver and told him I wanted to see him and he came in. I told him, Sandy, everything about what we believed he'd done to this family, what I did. After Dad's confession, well, I've been feeling more and more guilty about it all, especially as you lost your job through no fault of your own.'

'Sandy didn't lose her job,' Oliver pointedly put in. 'She resigned.'

'Well, it amounts to the same thing. She's out of work. Anyway, I finally decided I had to try and put things right.'

Oliver smiled warmly at the younger girl.

'It was a very brave thing to do, Lucy, and thank you. And remember what I said. You're worthy of someone better than Deakin.'

He glanced at Sandy at that point.

'Deakin's been dismissed, and I'm glad to say, Carrington's want to keep the whole thing quiet. Well, it doesn't reflect very well on them, does it? They simply extracted a promise from Deakin to leave town, which I believe he will be doing as soon as he's packed. I won't be taking any action either. What's done is done.'

He shrugged.

Lucy left the room at that point. The minute she'd gone, Sandy wished fervently for her back again. Oliver was looking at her in a very peculiar way, an expression upon his face that she didn't altogether trust.

'We need to talk,' he said, a purposeful smile playing about his mouth. 'Lucy told me you knew it was her who'd leaked the figures to Deakin. It's just like you to take the responsibility upon yourself but I wish you'd felt you could have confided in me. As it was, I suspected you weren't telling me everything. I just couldn't work out what it was, and then when you said it was totally down to you, well, I didn't know what to think. But, Sandy, we could have sorted things out. I would never have wanted to see Lucy in trouble. She's simply an easily-led teenager. We've all been there.'

Sandy just shrugged her shoulders. She didn't know what to say to him. She also couldn't bring herself to look at him. She was terrified of revealing her feelings and have him maybe laugh at her sheer presumption. She should have known she wouldn't get away with that.

'Sandy, look at me. I know that wall has some particularly fascinating aspects to it but — '

Knowing she had no choice, not really, she did as he asked.

'Please come back. I'm quite lost without you.'

Oliver's voice was gentle, low, full of a thrilling tenderness. As for his face, his eyes — Sandy couldn't believe the evidence of her own eyes, was afraid to believe what her senses were telling her. He couldn't feel the way she did, surely?

'Are you?'

The low words seemed wrung out of her.

'In more ways than you can possibly imagine.'

There was a gleam in his eye now, a provocative gleam. He was teasing her. Well, two could play that game.

'Tell me some of them.'

Sandy studied him from beneath her eyelashes. His look was sending out all sorts of crazy messages. Her heartbeat went into overdrive as he got to his feet and strode across to her.

'You know, don't you?'

'I want you to tell me,' she said softly.

'Come here first.'

He held his arms out to her, and she went straight into them, gladly, unhesitatingly. For the very first time in all of their dealings together, it felt right, her being there. He held her close and buried his face in her hair, his breath was warm against her skin.

'I've wanted you since the first moment I saw you.'

'Only wanted?' she provocatively asked.

He lifted his head and looked straight into her eyes.

'The loving came a short while later, the first time you stood there and gave me back as good as I was giving. I knew then I'd finally found the woman for me.'

'Oh, Oliver,' she sighed.

He kissed her then and Sandy surrendered herself totally to him. His arms tightened possessively round her.

'Why didn't you say something about your father and the way you all blamed me? I always sensed a stiffness, a holding back in you. I couldn't understand it. Your eyes said one thing but your body language said something else entirely.'

'Would you have told me the truth?' she asked, curiously.

'Well, no, but I'd have shifted heaven and earth to find your father and persuade him to tell you.'

Their lips met again in a kiss that went on and on.

'Enough of the past,' Oliver murmured eventually, 'the future's what matters now. So, Sandy Owen, will you let me court you, love you?'

Sandy couldn't see any point in holding back, not any longer.

'Oh, yes,' she breathed, 'yes, please.'

And Oliver gathered her even closer and kissed her with such longing, such passion, that her legs went quite weak with joy. She sagged against him. Oliver raised his head and looked down at her.

'You're not going to run away this time, are you?' he asked, his voice husky with emotion.

'Oh, no, you can be sure of that. I'm staying right where I am, with you.'

'For ever, I hope. It's where you belong, after all, my love. I think, deep down, you've always known that. I certainly have, and I've no intention of ever letting you go again.'

THE END

We do hope that you have enjoyed reading this large print book.

Did you know that all of our titles are available for purchase?

We publish a wide range of high quality large print books including:
Romances, Mysteries, Classics
General Fiction
Non Fiction and Westerns

Special interest titles available in large print are:
The Little Oxford Dictionary
Music Book, Song Book
Hymn Book, Service Book

Also available from us courtesy of Oxford University Press:
Young Readers' Dictionary
(large print edition)
Young Readers' Thesaurus
(large print edition)

For further information or a free brochure, please contact us at:
Ulverscroft Large Print Books Ltd.,
The Green, Bradgate Road, Anstey,
Leicester, LE7 7FU, England.
Tel: (00 44) **0116 236 4325**
Fax: (00 44) **0116 234 0205**